AN IMPERFECT LOVE

'Falling in love is where the trouble starts'

Divorce lawyer Justin Abernathy decided that when he got married it would not be determined by his heart—he had seen too much of romantic love turned sour. Alisa, whose experience of love had taught her a painful lesson, was sure that a marriage of convenience with no romantic frills would suit them both. Both were certain this was the right approach—until Alisa ruined the bargain they had made by falling in love with her new husband...

AN IMPERFECT LOVE

An Imperfect Love

by
Leigh Michaels

Magna Large Print Books
Long Preston, North Yorkshire,
England.

British Library Cataloguing in Publication Data.

Michaels, Leigh
 An imperfect love.

A catalogue record for this book is
available from the British Library

ISBN 0-7505-1210-5

First published in Great Britain by Mills & Boon Ltd., 1990

Copyright © 1990 by Leigh Michaels

Cover illustration © K. Ard by arrangement with Allied
Artists

The moral right of the author has been asserted

Published in Large Print 1998 by arrangement with Harlequin
Books SA

Magna Large Print is an imprint of
Library Magna Books Ltd.
Printed and bound in Great Britain by
T.J. International Ltd., Cornwall, PL28 8RW.

CHAPTER ONE

Traffic had been especially heavy on Camelback Road that morning, and it was just a little later than usual when Alisa parked her small car behind the sprawling masonry building that housed the firm of Harrison, Weber and Abernathy, Attorneys-at-Law. It was still early enough in the morning, however, for the sweater she had flung around her shoulders to be welcome. Phoenix might be more hospitable in early March than most other cities in the nation, but mornings and evenings could be crisp.

'Crisp,' she muttered to herself. 'You've lived in this climate for less than a year and you're already thoroughly spoiled. In Green Bay they're wading through snow-drifts three feet deep, and battling icy streets and cars that won't start in sub-zero weather. Meanwhile, you're complaining because you need a sweater in the morning!'

And sometimes, she thought, I'd gladly put up with the snow and the ice and the cold, if I could only go home...

She squared her shoulders. This is home now, she told herself. Home isn't a city or a neighbourhood or a house—it's a place where you are free to be yourself, without excuses, without play-acting, without having to hide behind a false smile. Home is where you can cry, if you need to, without having to explain.

And Green Bay could never be home to her again. Not as long as Shelley was there. Shelley, and Clay.

The receptionist looked up from the pile of mail she was sorting into neat little heaps and grinned. 'It isn't often that I'm here before you, Miss McClenaghan. Are you taking it easy this week, with Mr Abernathy out of town?'

Alisa smiled. 'Not exactly. Is that all his mail?'

The receptionist sneezed and shook her head. 'I don't think so. I seem to detect another scented one at the bottom of the pile.' She tossed a pale blue envelope on top of the stack. 'I know I shouldn't complain, because you usually sort out his mail. But how do you stand the conflicting perfumes? I think the job deserves combat pay, myself.' She sneezed again. 'I moved to Arizona to get away from the pollen, and now I find that perfume makes me weepy-eyed.'

'Not all Mr Abernathy's mail reeks of *Joy*.'

'No,' the receptionist agreed drily. 'Some of the ladies prefer *Sensually Meghan*. At five hundred dollars an ounce, I wouldn't think they'd waste it on notes to their divorce lawyer.'

Alisa laughed, in spite of herself. 'Be glad they're only writing him notes about their property settlements, instead of sitting around the reception-room all the time waiting to see him.'

The receptionist wrinkled her nose thoughtfully, and sniffed. 'I'll remember that. Still, after having been burned on matrimony once, you wouldn't think they'd

11

be eager to start flirting again.'

'Why not? For some of these women it's a way of life. Besides, you have to admit that he can certainly play the game.'

The receptionist looked scandalised. 'You don't mean that he would actually—?'

'I didn't say that,' Alisa reminded. But, she told herself, I've already said plenty that I shouldn't have said. She scooped up the stack of mail and carried it across the thick-carpeted reception-room to her own office, and shut the door firmly behind her.

A little of that kind of talk being overheard by the wrong person and you'll be out of a job, Alisa my girl, she told herself. No one, to her knowledge, had ever accused Justin Abernathy of misconduct with a client, and probably no one ever would. Using his phenomenally effective charm to cajole the ladies into co-operation was one thing, but he knew precisely where the line was drawn, and he would never step over it—at least, not as long as there was a divorce action pending. After the shouting was all over and the final papers were signed—well, that might be something else, she reflected. A number of his former clients seemed to hope that was the case, at any rate. And he had been seeing a lot of one of them, lately. But then Debbie Baxter knew how to play the game, too.

Alisa sighed and reached for the razor-sharp letter opener. Quickly, systematically, she slit the envelopes, and then unfolded each letter one by one, listed the contents in the mail log she kept faithfully up to date, and attached a note where necessary summarising the message the letter contained.

Eight months ago, when she had first come to work for Justin Abernathy, she had carefully sorted his mail and placed a stack of unopened envelopes on his desk blotter each morning. All of them were marked 'Personal' or 'Private' or 'Confidential'. Most of them were addressed in a feminine hand. She had felt a little strange about even handling them, as if she was violating his privacy.

On the fourth morning of her employment he had summoned her into his office and pointed at the pile she had put on his desk just minutes before. 'What are those doing here?' he had asked.

'I assumed, since they're marked "Personal", Mr Abernathy, that you wanted—'

'Mail which comes to my office is, by definition, not personal,' he had said.

Alisa had blinked at him in astonishment. 'You can't mean that you want me to deal with those?'

He had leaned back in his big leather chair and clasped his hands at the base of his neck and said, sounding honestly curious, 'Why not? You're a confidential secretary, aren't you?'

She hadn't been able to argue with that. So she had taken the stack of envelopes back to her desk and, with trepidation, opened them. It had become easier over the months, and now she didn't even look to see what warnings were written on the envelopes. He'd been right—the vast majority were business, after all. The occasional exception had ceased to embarrass her; it certainly never seemed to bother Justin Abernathy...

She glanced at the legal pad on the corner of her desk, waiting patiently for her to finish with the mail. The list of things to do filled an entire page in neat shorthand. The fact that Justin Abernathy had been in Flagstaff for most of the week taking depositions for a big divorce case didn't mean that his secretary was having an easy time of it in Phoenix; as usual, things had become even more frantic the instant he'd stepped out of the office. And it didn't matter where he went, either. As long as Justin Abernathy was within reach of a telephone, Alisa wouldn't lack for things to keep her busy. She was half amused at the receptionist's idea that she was having a vacation with him gone all week. What did the girl think Alisa did behind her closed office door all day anyway? File her nails? Play solitaire? Tap-dance on the polished mahogany top of her desk?

At any rate, that sort of thing might be the receptionist's idea of a pleasant day at the office, but it wasn't Alisa's. As a good secretary, she prided herself on her efficient use of time...

'Oh, stop patting yourself on the back for being virtuous,' she told herself crossly. 'You're just edgy because it's Friday and you haven't any idea what you're going to do with the whole weekend. Well, tonight you'll just have to get busy and plan something—anything—to fill up all those hours. Then you'll feel better.'

She picked up the last envelope. It was addressed in a spidery, cramped hand that she recognised instantly; Justin Abernathy had received a letter from his great-aunt Louise every Friday morning for the entire eight months Alisa had worked for him. She had wondered at first how Louise Abernathy managed such consistency, considering the vagaries of the postal service. But then, as the letters continued and she got to know Louise a little better, it became obvious. No one would dare to contradict Louise's wishes, not even the federal government. The only exception was apparently Justin Abernathy, and even he had learned not to push certain subjects with her.

For example, the telephone system.

Louise believed the telephone was an invention of the devil, and she was certain that anyone who used it for anything short of dire emergency was inevitably going to be struck down by lightning. Not even Justin could change her mind on that and so every Monday Alisa mailed a letter from Justin to Louise. He never wrote the letters, of course; Alisa did. Sometimes she wondered if he even bothered to read them any more before he signed his name.

This week Louise's letter was enclosed in a birthday card, along with a generous-sized cheque. Alisa looked at the card with surprise, and then laughed at herself. 'Did you think the man didn't have birthdays?' she asked herself lightly. Well, his secret was out now; Justin Abernathy would be thirty-five tomorrow, and his great-aunt Louise wasn't about to let him forget it.

Alisa chewed thoughtfully on her pen as she deciphered Louise's handwriting. It was going to take a bit of tact to answer this one properly, she reflected. Oh, well—it would give her something to think about all weekend. She put the letter

17

on the corner of her desk so she wouldn't forget to take it home with her.

She skipped lunch and used the time instead to drop off some papers at the court-house. It wasn't that she didn't trust the messenger service, but sometimes she preferred the secure feeling of putting important documents into the right hands herself. Besides, she told herself, it made a good excuse to get out of the office, and, though driving in Phoenix traffic at high noon was hardly a heavenly experience, the view of the mountains that surrounded the Valley of the Sun certainly made up for it. The palm-lined streets, with gigantic saguaro and barrel cacti standing proudly at unexpected intervals, were part of a landscape that still looked surreal to a girl who had grown up in the woods of northern Wisconsin. She had to remind herself at least once a day that Phoenix was not just an enormous film set.

The receptionist greeted her on her return with a stack of yellow message slips. 'Mr Coltrain is here, too,' she said, as Alisa shuffled expertly through the memos.

'I told him you'd be back any minute, so he said he'd wait.'

Alisa's fingers clenched on a yellow square. For an instant, she stared down at it, and then put it at the bottom of the pile. Her fingers were trembling a little. 'I hope you didn't let him into my office.'

'No, he's in the conference-room drinking coffee. Are you all right, Miss McClenaghan?'

Alisa smiled absently. 'Of course. I was just thinking about the files I'd left on my desk. We wouldn't want to let anybody from a rival firm get a look at those, would we?'

The receptionist looked puzzled, but before she could answer Alisa had crossed the carpeted reception-room.

Dumb, she told herself. Very, very dumb. Everyone in the firm knows what a stickler you are about locking everything up before you leave, even if it's only to go and have a cup of coffee in the employees' lounge. There is nothing on your desk at all—certainly nothing of a sensitive nature. Ridge Coltrain could spend weeks in there

19

and not come up with anything that would help him next time he goes up against Mr Abernathy in court.

But letting the receptionist think she was upset about Ridge Coltrain was better than the alternative. She closed her eyes for an instant, and the image of the yellow message slip seemed to be burned on to the back of her eyelids. 'Shelley called,' it said. 'Said it is urgent; please call her back as soon as possible.'

That was all. There was no reason why anyone should suspect that simple message of making Alisa's heart race and her insides feel strangely empty.

It's Clay, she thought. Something must have happened to Clay...

And until she had dealt with business there was absolutely nothing she could do about Shelley's call, so she squared her shoulders and went down the hall to the conference-room.

Ridge Coltrain was leaning back in the leather chair at the head of the long table, a coffee-mug dangling from his hand, dreamily studying the modern-art print that nearly filled the opposite wall.

'Sorry to keep you waiting, Ridge,' Alisa said crisply. 'You're here for the papers on the Goulds' property settlement, right?'

He uncoiled himself from the chair, stretching lazily to his full height, which was considerable. 'I'm in no hurry,' he murmured. 'I love to sit and absorb the atmosphere of this place. If it's true that you can tell a successful lawyer by the expensive furniture in his office, then Justin obviously has no worries.'

Alisa bit back a smile. Ridge Coltrain's law practice was a new one, and not the most secure as yet, but there was no envy in his voice, only idle good humour. That self-control, she had heard Justin Abernathy say, was precisely why the young man was going to be dangerous in a courtroom when he got a little more experience under his belt.

If Ridge Coltrain ever heard that, she thought, he would probably take it as a compliment—and understandably so. But he would never hear it from her.

She led the way into the office and

21

unlocked the bottom drawer of her desk. 'I expected that you'd send your secretary over.'

'My secretary can't be trusted to get herself to work on time, much less clear across Phoenix with a set of important papers. Are you sure you don't want a job, Alisa? I can't pay you what Justin does, that's sure, but think of the challenge.' He waved his mug in the air. 'And you wouldn't have to wash fancy china cups, either—we use the plastic foam kind.'

'Sorry to disappoint you, Ridge, but the cleaning service does the mugs.' Please, she thought, just take the papers and go, Ridge. I don't want to chat today...

He shook his head sadly. 'You have no sense of adventure, Alisa.' He flipped the folder open and ran a finger down a page. 'I'll look at this over the weekend and get back to Justin next week. And if you change your mind about wanting a job...'

She smiled and said everything that was pleasant, and hurried him out of the door as quickly as she could without being rudely obvious. The instant the door closed behind him she grabbed for the telephone.

There was no answer at Shelley's apartment.

Alisa reached for the message slip again; there was no telephone number on it. How like Shelley, she thought, to say it's urgent and then not leave a number where she can be reached! Shall I try the hospitals? Or the police, perhaps?

Don't be a fool, she told herself sternly. You don't know that anything is truly wrong; remember that everything Shelley ever wanted was urgent. And you have a job to do, anyway—you can't spend the afternoon on the telephone trying to run down every emergency facility in Green Bay to ask if something *might* have happened!

But she kept trying every half-hour, and listening to the dull buzz of an unanswered telephone in an empty apartment. And every time her own phone rang her pulse leaped until she found that it was not Shelley.

By mid-afternoon, with the continual

interruptions of the telephone—every one of Justin Abernathy's clients seemed to be having a crisis this week, she told herself wearily—she had worked her way only halfway down her list of things to do. Perhaps, she thought, Louise Abernathy had a point after all. The world would be a much more civilised place without the continual demanding chime of a telephone.

That was when Debbie Baxter strolled into the office, swinging a pair of sunglasses between her thumb and forefinger. She was wearing faultless white tennis shorts that showed off her perfectly tanned legs to an almost indecent height. Her tightly fitted top also displayed a great deal of Debbie in a slightly different way, and her long red hair tumbled wildly around her shoulders. Alisa concluded that it had been artfully arranged; to the average man, she thought, it would probably look as if Debbie had just come off the court. She looked a good ten years younger than her real age, which Alisa happened to know because Debbie's divorce had still been pending when Alisa had first come to work for Justin Abernathy.

I must have another chat with the receptionist, Alisa told herself. People aren't supposed to just wander into my office like this. But then, she thought, Debbie Baxter didn't consider herself to be any ordinary person. It would take more than a receptionist to stop her.

Debbie's eyes went eagerly to Justin's office, and her face fell when she saw the open door and the darkened room beyond.

'He's still in Flagstaff,' Alisa said, without waiting to be asked.

Debbie curled up in the chair beside Alisa's desk, as lithe and supple as a jungle cat. Or a python, Alisa thought.

'He isn't going to be up there all weekend, is he?'

'He hasn't told me, but I doubt it.' Alisa didn't take her eyes off the legal pad where she was summarising the questions of the last client who had called.

'He'd better not. We have a date for tomorrow.'

'I'm sure he wouldn't miss it.'

Debbie looked at her for a long moment, as if suspecting irony, and then confided, 'Well, it's a bit difficult, you see. It's just sort of a casual date—I mean, I let him think it was nothing important because I didn't want him to be suspicious, but I'm really having a surprise party for him, for his birthday.'

Alisa's eyebrows went up. Obviously I was wrong, she thought. His birthday is apparently no big secret, after all.

'He hasn't a clue, and I can hardly call him up in Flagstaff and make a big production out of asking when he's coming home.'

'I wouldn't recommend that, no.'

Debbie looked expectantly across the desk, and said finally, 'You could find out for me.'

Alisa sighed. Refusing would obviously do her no good; telling Debbie no and making it stick took about the same effort as wearing down a rock with a trickle of water. 'If he calls the office, I will remind him to check his calendar for the weekend.'

Debbie thought that over. 'I suppose I'll have to be content with that.'

'I'm afraid it's the best I can do.'

'I know,' Debbie said sympathetically. 'He'd get suspicious if his secretary suddenly wanted to know all about his weekend plans. I mean, it's obviously none of your concern what he does with his free time.' She frowned, and then added suddenly, 'But if you do this favour for me, the next time I get a chance I'll introduce you to my ex-husband. You'd make a great couple.'

Alisa bit her lip and said, choking only slightly, 'Thank you. But—'

'Bob always seemed to like the dowdy, efficient secretarial type. That's mainly why we got divorced.' She glanced towards the door; then a glow spread over her face and she sat up eagerly. 'Justin! I thought you were never going to get home!'

From the corner of her eye, Alisa could see wariness spring to life in the dark brown eyes of the man in the doorway. That was a bad tactical mistake, Debbie, she thought. The last thing you want is for him to recognise that he's being pursued...

Debbie seemed to realise it too. She glanced at the delicate watch strapped to her wrist and said, 'Goodness, it's late. I must be going, Justin, dear. I only stopped in to tell your secretary that I think she should meet Bob. Don't you agree? They're exactly the same type.' She stood on her toes and kissed his cheek. 'Oh, we are still playing tennis tomorrow, aren't we? Silly me—I'd almost forgotten.'

Alisa gave her points for the fast recovery. Perhaps the woman wasn't as dizzy as she sounded after all.

Justin Abernathy was frowning. 'Debbie, I'm really swamped with work—'

She straightened his tie and pouted prettily. 'Justin, dear, you mustn't work all the time, you know—it makes you a very dull boy. And we can't disappoint the Buchanans. They're counting on us, and they'll only be here for another week.'

'I suppose you're right.'

Debbie smiled triumphantly and blew

Alisa an elaborate kiss from the doorway. 'Do remember what I said about Bob, darling. I'll be delighted to introduce you. It's so sensible to be friends with one's ex, you know, and I'd love to see him get the—happiness he deserves.'

Alisa couldn't decide whether to laugh or cry. She settled for closing her eyes for a long instant, and by the time she opened them Justin Abernathy had crossed the room and turned on the lights in his office. 'If you're not too busy dreaming about Bob Baxter, Mac,' he said from the doorway, as he pulled his tie loose, 'I'd like to get some work done.' He didn't wait for an answer.

Alisa smothered a sigh and gathered up the mail, the stack of messages and her notebook. She had been 'Miss McClenaghan' for the first two days she had worked for him; then, in a busy moment, he had called for 'Mac' and she had made the mistake of answering. It wasn't that she minded, exactly. Most of the time she thoroughly enjoyed working for him, and even the nickname didn't bother her. It was only at times like this, when the pace got busy and tense and he lost his sense of humour, that being called 'Mac' really annoyed her.

He had shed his jacket and tie and was emptying the contents of his calfskin briefcase on to his desk when she came in; he looked up and watched as she came across the room.

She tried not to let the inspection bother her, but Debbie's words seemed to echo in her mind. 'The dowdy, efficient secretarial type', she had said. Was that what Justin Abernathy was thinking, too? Alisa's soft olive-green dress was well-tailored, but its lines were classic rather than high fashion, intended to fade into the background. Her make-up was understated, her thick ash-blonde hair fell in unfashionably straight lines to her shoulders, and the glasses she wore when she was reading weren't an accessory, but a necessity. Still, it was scarcely fair to call her dowdy...

In any case, she told herself firmly, my salary isn't large enough for me to be a trend-setter, so he can hardly complain if

I don't look like one.

She squared her shoulders and sat down beside his desk. 'Where would you like to begin, Mr Abernathy?' she asked woodenly.

He looked at her for a long moment. 'Forget my temper tantrum, will you, Mac? It's been a long day.'

'I'm sorry to hear that. Not the depositions, I hope?'

'No—that went well. But I dictated notes all the way back from Flagstaff, and it wasn't until I was within twenty miles of Phoenix that I discovered the damned tape recorder wasn't working. And I'd just put new batteries in it, too.' He tossed the recorder on to the shelf of a bookcase and smiled suddenly. 'Sorry—I shouldn't take it out on you.'

She thought she had learned, in eight months, to brace herself against that smile; the impact of it was roughly similar to a tidal wave. But she found herself saying, 'Perhaps if you were to try again while it's still fresh in your mind—'

'Dictate it all to you right now, you

mean? That was a four-hour drive.' He finished taking folders out of the briefcase, snapped it shut and set it aside. 'No, I'd hate to make you cancel a date tonight, Mac. I'll just take another recorder home for the weekend.'

She wasn't going to argue with him, and neither was she eager to admit that there was no date to be cancelled. Besides, she thought, what he had really meant was that he had no intention of cancelling his! She glanced at the top message in the stack. 'Mr Johnson went to pick up his kids for visitation last night and there was no one at home...'

It was nearly thirty minutes later when she said, 'And Mrs Morrison wrote to say that she's thought it over very hard, but, despite what she agreed to do last week, she couldn't live with herself if she let her husband take the Pekinese.'

Justin Abernathy rubbed his knuckles against his jaw. 'Astounding,' he said. 'They can agree on the house, the kids, the cars and the bank accounts, but when it comes to a ten-year-old Pekinese dog everything breaks down.'

'Chu Lin will be twelve next month,' Alisa murmured. 'It's here on page five of the letter, right where she sprayed the perfume. *Midnight Passion*, I think—' She caught the gleam in his eyes and said, 'Sorry.'

'Visitation rights for a dog—you know, Mac, when I first started in this business I'd have laughed about the possibility of that sort of thing dragging me into court. I'll have to call her and see what we can work out. Is that everything?'

Alisa picked up the last envelope, stretched her cramped fingers and said, 'All the official stuff. But your Aunt Louise sent you a birthday card.'

He groaned and reached across the desk for it. 'Does the woman never forget?'

'Would Emily Post?' Alisa asked crisply.

He glanced at the cheque, raised his eyebrows, laid it aside and picked up the letter. 'I'll bet Emily Post wouldn't say this kind of thing to her favourite great-nephew, just because he's not married yet.'

'I'm sure Louise thinks it's her duty.'

'I don't see why. *She* never got married.' He turned the letter a little and squinted at the spidery handwriting. 'And as for telling me that she'd rather have a visit from my wife next Christmas instead of another knickknack to dust—'

'That hurt my feelings,' Alisa said. 'It was a handmade porcelain bluebird that I sent her, and it cost you the earth.'

'Don't remind me. I saw the bill.'

'She is your only great-aunt; you can't be cheap about these things. Still, there are limits, and she seems to have reached yours. Would you like me to draft a reply?'

He lowered the letter and looked at her over the edge of it with considerable interest. 'Just what would you tell her? I've already suggested that she mind her own business—several times over the last ten years.'

'I wouldn't do that, exactly. There are more tactful ways.'

'Such as? You intrigue me, Mac—no one has ever managed anything of the sort with Louise.'

'Oh, I could explain to her how dealing with broken marriages every day has soured you on the idea altogether, and that her nagging will only remind you of all the frustrated ex-wives you have to deal with—'

'So far, so good.'

'And if she keeps it up she'll make you glad that you can go home alone every night. Well,' Alisa added with a pang of conscience, 'perhaps not *alone*, but there's no need to tell Aunt Louise that, surely—?'

He dropped the letter and leaned back in his chair with a burst of laughter. 'I think you're right—we should draw the line at the nagging ex-wives. By the way, is that patriotic fervour I hear in your voice, Mac? You sound a bit disillusioned yourself.'

Alisa shrugged. 'I was just trying to help.' She drew a tiny design on the margin of her notebook and looked up. 'Besides, I thought you really felt that way. You certainly say often enough that love is blind.'

He nodded. 'And marriage is an institution for the blind. I know. Don't quote me any more, I can't handle it.' He glanced at the letter again and put it back in the envelope. 'If you can pull this one off, Mac, I'll give you a rise and promote you to writing the briefs for all my appeals.' He ran a hand over the back of his neck. A stray late-afternoon sunbeam touched his head, turning his rumpled brown hair almost auburn for an instant. 'I think that's all for now.' His voice was abstracted, and he opened a folder and reached for a yellow pad and a pen.

Alisa smiled wryly. She—and Great-Aunt Louise—had been abruptly consigned to oblivion, that was for sure. She gathered up the rest of the mail and slipped quietly out of his office, closing the door softly behind her.

She had lost track of time when it opened again. She looked up from the typewriter in surprise; he halted in the doorway, obviously just as startled to see her, with his briefcase in one hand and his jacket slung over his shoulder. 'I thought I told you not to cancel your date, Mac.'

She nervously pushed her glasses up. 'It wasn't important. I didn't want to let all this wait till Monday.'

He looked at the wire basket on the corner of her desk, full of neatly typed legal documents, and the stack of letters, each clipped to its envelope, waiting for his signature.

'Well, it's time to go home now.' He snapped the lights off in his office.

She glanced at the clock on the credenza behind her desk. 'I didn't realise it was so late. I still have this letter to finish, so I'll lock up.'

He set his briefcase on a chair. He looked a little exasperated. 'Go home, Mac. Whoever is waiting for you is going to think I'm a slave-driver, and I hate having my reputation maligned for no good reason.'

His voice was faintly ironic, but that wasn't what brought the stinging tears to her eyes. It was, instead, the memory of last winter, when there had been someone waiting for her at home, a bit jealous of the time that her work absorbed...

Don't be foolish, she told herself. Clay never exactly hung around the apartment waiting for you; it was more the other way around. And you're only thinking about him so much today because of Shelley's call. Damn the girl, anyway; she still wasn't answering her telephone...

Alisa swallowed hard and said, with a carefully cheerful note, 'Really, I'd rather finish the letters.'

He leaned across the desk and tugged at a bright-coloured scrap of paper that peeked out of her desk drawers. 'And I suppose this is what you call dinner,' he said, waving the remains of a chocolate bar under her nose. 'Milk chocolate and almonds do not make a balanced meal.' He broke off a piece and ate it thoughtfully. 'Get your coat, Mac. I'm going to take you to Emilio's Bar and Grill and feed you.'

'I shouldn't—' I should go home, she thought, but surely not even Shelley would expect me to sit by the telephone and wait?

I've already tried a dozen times to call her back.

He looked her over thoughtfully. 'Why? *Is* someone waiting for you?'

'Tonight, only the cat.' Despite her best efforts, she knew she sounded tired.

'Then don't argue with me. I don't know about the state of your refrigerator, but I can guess.' He finished off the chocolate bar and tossed the wrapper at the waste-paper basket. 'Half a can of left-over tuna for the cat, right?'

She smiled in spite of herself.

'And the only thing I'm likely to find in mine tonight is the green mould that's been growing all week. You wouldn't condemn me to that, would you? Besides, I hate going to restaurants alone.'

She bit her tongue to keep from answering that one. 'Doesn't your house-keeper keep the kitchen stocked?'

'I don't have one any more.'

'But I hired—'

'Three, wasn't it? They don't seem to last,' he said blithely. 'They all say the house is too big and I'm too impossible,

39

and I thought if I asked you to try again you might resign. I can do without a housekeeper, but...'

Alisa shuddered a little. When she stopped to consider it, she couldn't think of anyone who had set foot inside Justin Abernathy's house in the four months he'd owned it. Now, she suspected, she knew why.

'They all seem to detest clutter,' he went on. 'They don't understand that that's why I bought a big house in the first place—so I don't have to worry about the clutter. Now stop trying to distract me and let's go eat.'

She found herself standing on the pavement, clutching her handbag and sweater, while he locked the door. He tossed his briefcase into the back of the bright red Cadillac convertible that was snuggled against the building. 'I'll follow you—there's no sense in coming all the way back across town to pick up your car.' The Cadillac's engine roared to life.

She sighed and pulled her car keys out of her handbag, and thought briefly about driving off in the other direction. But there was no sense in making a scene; she had to eat, after all. As for Shelley—well, another hour certainly couldn't make any difference. And not even Debbie Baxter could raise much of a fuss about a man taking his secretary out for something to eat after a late night's work.

Of course, Alisa thought, if it had been Debbie they'd have left her car here no matter how far they were going, and she'd have nestled down in the front seat of the Cadillac and let her hair blow wildly in the wind...

'And he says he hates going to restaurants alone,' she muttered. 'I wonder how he could possibly know!'

CHAPTER TWO

Emilio's Bar and Grill was in a dark little shop-front in a less-than-attractive neighbourhood. Alisa parked her car on the street behind the Cadillac and looked warily at the building. The front window was full of neon signs that advertised various brands of beer, and the day's special was scrawled in yellow chalk on an untidy green board propped on the pavement. It looked like a dive. It certainly didn't impress her as the sort of place the elegantly tailored Justin Abernathy would frequent.

At the moment, however, he wasn't quite as elegant as usual. He was leaning against his car waiting for her, with his arms folded across his chest; he had put his jacket back on, but his tie was nowhere to be seen.

He saw her glance doubtfully up at the

creaking sign above the door. 'You've never been here before, have you?' he asked.

'How did you manage to guess?' Alisa said crisply. 'This looks like the kind of place I usually cross the street to avoid.'

He laughed. 'I keep forgetting you're not a native, Mac. Wait till you see what you've been missing.'

Inside, high-backed booths lined the walls, and tables surrounded a tiny, battered dance-floor. Along one wall stretched a long bar, and in the corner a battered juke-box beat out a strong rhythm. The décor ran to vinyl, paper and cheap heavy glass. But she couldn't help noticing that every surface was spotlessly clean, and the smells that issued forth from somewhere in the back were heavenly.

He guided her to a booth in the corner furthest from the juke-box. 'Emilio's is one of the best-kept secrets in Phoenix,' he said. 'It's sort of a conspiracy among the natives—if too many tourists start frequenting the place, Emilio might be tempted to change things to please them.'

'And that would ruin it for the regulars, I suppose?'

'You bet it would. Spruce up the surroundings and all the charm would be gone. As it is—well, I was here one night when a guy came in and asked to see the wine list. Emilio looked at him as if he'd come from another planet and said, "I have white and red—you want me to write it down?"'

Alisa giggled.

Justin Abernathy waved a hand at a hand-painted poster above the booth. 'I think that's enough of a violation of tradition, myself. Serving green beer for St Patrick's Day at Emilio's, of all places—'

'It doesn't seem to fit, that's true.'

'You Irishmen have taken over the world.' He sounded a bit grumpy about it.

'Don't blame me. My branch of the McClenaghans is Scottish.' The waitress started towards them, and Alisa added, under her breath, 'Does the place have a menu, or is it like the wine list—stored in Emilio's head?'

He laughed. 'All the regulars have it memorised.'

'Then you can order for me. I hate looking like a tourist.'

'It's easy, really. Just tell her how you want your steak cooked—the rest comes automatically.'

He smiled approvingly when she said medium rare. Alisa couldn't help but notice that the waitress didn't ask how he wanted his steak prepared; obviously it wasn't only the customers who had things memorised at Emilio's.

'There,' he said with satisfaction after the woman brought their drinks and went away. 'It's not busy, so the food won't take long. I always did think the worst thing about Emilio's was having to breathe the aromas while you wait—it's sheer torture when you're hungry.' He sipped his margarita and looked across the table. 'No one has told you about Emilio's? What kind of people do you hang around with, anyway, Mac? Obviously not the natives.'

'For a long time I didn't think there were any natives—it seems that everyone who lives in Phoenix came here from somewhere else.'

He nodded. 'Snowbirds who move south to avoid the harsh winters. Like you. We can't all be lucky enough to be born here.'

'That wasn't why I came,' she said, before she stopped to think. 'I love winter, really.'

He looked less than convinced. 'That's easy to say, when you're down here basking in the sunshine. I've spent a few winters up north myself, and it isn't the charming scene that Christmas carols make it sound like.'

'Of course it isn't. For one thing, chestnuts roasted on an open fire don't taste all that good. But there is something bracing about a long walk when it's so cold that the snow squeaks under your feet.'

He shuddered. 'The best thing I found about winter in Michigan was electric socks.'

'Electric *socks?* What a pansy— Sorry.'

He was grinning. 'That's all right, Mac. Don't go prim and proper on me now.

Actually, there was one other thing I liked about cold weather—it was easier to talk a girl into snuggling up with me when she was half frozen.'

Alisa bit her lip.

'It was a lesson I never forgot,' he added gently. 'But now I just turn the heating down, and I can accomplish the same thing right here in Arizona.'

She tried her best to ignore that one. 'What on earth were you doing in Michigan, anyway? If you hate the cold—'

'Law school. I went up to look at the campus in the fall, and it was very pleasant. I didn't stop to think what it would be like in February with the wind howling straight down from the Arctic Circle. There's one thing about hot weather—you can always cool yourself off. But there were days that I thought I'd never get my bones warm again.'

Alisa was shaking her head. 'Oh, no. It's the other way around. Cavemen used to stay put in the winter and huddle around the fire, but do you know what they did

47

in the summer? They moved to a more bearable climate—'

'That's the most original anthropological argument I've ever heard, and the most ridiculous. But let's get back to real-life cases. If you didn't come to Phoenix to worship the sun, then what did bring you here?'

'It was time for a change. So I threw a dart at the map of the United States, and this was where it landed.' She said it with a perfectly straight face, knowing that he would never suspect how close it was to the truth.

'I'd say giving up Green Bay for Phoenix qualifies as a change, all right. Not that I'm complaining, you understand—I've certainly benefited from having you around. How long has it been?'

'Eight months.' Alisa moved her margarita glass so the waitress could set a platter in front of her. It contained an enormous, thick steak smothered in onions and green peppers, surrounded by a wreath of golden-brown sauté potatoes. The steak was still hissing gently from the heat of the grill. She picked up her knife; the meat was so tender that the weight of the blade was enough to cut through it.

'That long? And you still have only a cat waiting for you when you go home at night?'

'Why would you think I should have—?'

'You didn't cancel a date tonight, did you, Mac?'

The suddenness of the question startled her into honesty. 'No, I didn't, but that doesn't mean—' She stopped abruptly. I'm beginning to know how it feels to be cross-examined, she thought.

He shook his head sadly. 'I thought by now you would have got over the klutz in Green Bay.'

Alisa put down her knife carefully. Her hand shook a little. 'The klutz in Green Bay?' she repeated icily.

'The guy who broke your heart. Jeff told me—'

'Jeff?' Her voice was rising.

'Are you setting up in business as an echo, or what? You can't have forgotten Jeff; he was your boss.'

'Jeff told you about—' She caught herself, and bit her lip hard. But it was too late for denial, so she added tartly, 'I ought to sue him for violating my confidence.'

He shook his head. 'You can't, unless you were actually a client. And don't blame Jeff. He probably wouldn't have said anything at all, but we were law-school classmates, so of course when I asked—'

His tone was meant to be soothing, but it had no such effect on Alisa.

'That's not exactly a consolation,' she said sharply. 'I thought he was trying to help me out when he said that if I insisted on coming to Phoenix I should ask you for a job—'

'Yes, and he told me that if he had to lose the best legal secretary he'd ever found, I might as well benefit. When I asked him why such a good secretary was leaving him, he told me that you'd been wounded in the battle of the heart and needed a place to heal. What did you do, fall in love with him?'

She swallowed an ice-cube unexpectedly,

and choked. 'Of course I didn't fall in love with him. Jeff is my friend, or at least he used to be, before he started talking about me like this!'

'Don't get mad at him. I didn't give him much of a choice, actually.'

'Oh?' She was beginning to sound dangerous.

'Well, women like you don't just leave a secure job with a boss like Jeff Winslow and trail halfway across the country for the fun of it; there had to be a reason, and I wanted to know what it was before I hired you.'

'So you've known all this time?'

'Well, he didn't give me the details. But even if he hadn't told me, it was elementary once I got to know you a bit better. You're not the sort who gets into financial trouble. It couldn't have been legal problems, or Jeff wouldn't have given you a reference. That leaves men—or rather, a man. I don't think you're the sort to have a string of them, either.'

Words failed her. It took a couple of minutes to find her voice. 'This is a fascinating dissection of my personality problems,' she said stiffly, 'but I can't imagine why you think it's any of your business, Mr Abernathy!'

It didn't stop him. 'Why are you so upset that he told me?'

'Because it's private, dammit!'

His eyebrows went up. 'Such language, Mac,' he said gently. 'And anything that affects your performance as an employee isn't totally private—'

'It has nothing to do with my job.'

'If you didn't fall in love with your boss, then what was it, anyway? A particularly messy divorce? Considering some of the things I've heard you say about marriage, Mac—'

'It wasn't a divorce. Why do you want to know, anyway?'

'Professional curiosity,' he said promptly.

'That's absolutely ghoulish! If you're so terribly curious, why wait till now? Why haven't you asked any time in the last eight months?'

'Because I'd almost forgotten about it,' he admitted, 'till I called Jeff this week about the arrangements for our law-school reunion next summer and he asked how you were doing, and if you'd got over your broken heart yet. I told him I didn't know, but I'd look into it.'

'I'm going to send him a letter-bomb,' Alisa muttered.

He propped his elbows on the table and looked expectantly across at her. 'All right, if it wasn't a divorce, what in hell did this guy do to you? If you've given up dating altogether—'

'I didn't say I never date, Mr Abernathy. I said I hadn't cancelled a date tonight—'

'You certainly made it sound as if you're off men forever, Mac.'

Goaded past all endurance, she snapped, 'My name is not Mac!'

He blinked. Then, gently, he said, 'Mine isn't *Mr* Abernathy, either, and the title is as out of place in a friendly conversation like this—'

'This is a friendly conversation?'

'—as a wine list is at Emilio's. When I think about it, if you could call Jeff by his first name there's no reason why you should insist on being formal with me.'

'I haven't been invited to do anything else.'

He smiled. 'Now you have.' He cut another bite from his steak and said, 'Your reluctance to tell me what happened only encourages me to speculate, you know—Alisa.'

She sighed. It would also encourage him to call up Jeff Winslow, who might tell him anything at all. And Jeff, who had been her friend as well as her employer, knew very nearly everything there was to know about her—and Clay. 'All right, just to save you the trouble of asking again, I'll tell you what happened. The man I loved married—' she stopped, and then said quietly '—someone else.'

He looked doubtful. 'That's all?'

She started to tell him that to any sane person that would be more than enough. Then she caught herself. 'Yes, that's all. Petty of me, isn't it, to be hurt by a little thing like that?'

'I don't think Jeff would be too happy

to hear that you're still hiding in a cave, Mac.'

She bit her tongue. Obviously, he didn't even know what he'd called her; old habits died hard. 'I'm not hiding.'

'I don't know about that. Eight months of mourning sounds like—'

'And I'm not mourning! I've simply chosen not to get involved with another man just now, and maybe not ever. I should think you'd applaud that sentiment; surely after a few years in your profession you can't believe that everyone is cut out for marriage?'

He grinned. 'Well, the universal desire to be half of a couple certainly provides job security for me. Is that why he married someone else? Because you didn't think you were suited for marriage?'

She pushed her plate away, picked up her margarita, and said resignedly, 'I should have known you weren't finished discussing my personal problems, Mr—'

He frowned.

Alisa said sweetly, 'I'd forgotten—Justin.' It felt strange, as if she was having to twist her tongue around a set of foreign vowels.

'That doesn't fit, you know,' he said. 'Women—and you must admit I am an expert of sorts on the female species—'

'Of sorts, yes,' she murmured.

'Are you being sarcastic, Mac? Sorry—*Alisa.* Women who are opposed to marriage usually want careers instead. They want to be the lawyer, not the legal secretary.'

'I never said I was opposed to marriage itself. I'd have been good at it, too.' To her dismay, there was a tiny break in her voice. She tried to cover it up with a flippant twist. 'I always liked baking chocolate-chip cookies.'

He didn't comment for a long time, and when he did it surprised her. 'True love rarely seems to end in true happiness,' he said. 'And the search for it does incredible damage to human lives.'

She had no trouble remembering a few cases like that herself, where one person's search for romance had broken families, destroyed careers, wiped out fortunes. Well, she thought, it's no wonder if both of us have a slightly jaundiced view of romance, just because of the sort of things we see every day.

'At any rate, once that sort of love comes and goes there doesn't seem to be much sense in continuing to search.' She kept her voice firm with an effort. 'That's a fact of life that simply has to be accepted, and I've done that.'

He swirled the ice in his glass and said thoughtfully, 'Things might change. The klutz might—'

She shook her head. 'Not likely. In any case, do you think I'd want a man who would leave his wife for me? I've seen too many situations of that sort, and they never turn out well. I have a little more self-esteem than that.'

But not much more, she thought, if I'm being truly honest. Clay didn't leave me with much. He didn't even have the decency to tell me himself that he was going to be married...

Enough of that, she told herself. 'I guess I was never very realistic anyway,' she said. 'For one thing, I'd want kids—several kids.

I don't believe in inflicting single, spoilt children on the world. And I want to be at home with them when they're little. It seems to me that there isn't much point in having a family at all unless someone is willing to make that sacrifice—to give up a job for a while for the sake of the kids. Remember the Abbots?'

He nodded.

'I'm not blaming her for what happened, but she was so busy being a high-powered professional woman that I can understand why he fell in love with the nanny.'

'The women's movement will burn you in effigy, Mac.'

'I don't see why they should. They're fighting for women to have the right to make choices. I think staying at home to raise responsible human beings is a perfectly valid choice.'

'So when can I expect your resignation, so you can put this plan into effect?'

It was quiet, but the reminder hit her like a blow to the stomach. Those dreams could never come true for her now.

And before you start feeling depressed

about it, Alisa, she reminded herself, remember that even if things had worked out differently with Clay you couldn't have put your dream entirely into practice. It wouldn't have been easy to make ends meet on his salary alone; you would have had to keep working.

'I'm not going to resign,' she said steadily. 'I said that's what I'd have liked—not what I'm planning to do.'

'So what are you going to do instead?'

'Well, I'm not going to law school either.' She smiled. 'And you can tell Jeff next time you talk to him that I'm quite happy where I am.'

'Tell him yourself. I don't think he'll believe me.'

'I can't think why he wouldn't. Jeff must know that once you make up your mind to get to the bottom of something, you do it—even if it takes thumbscrews.'

He grinned. 'The reputation for persistence has followed me,' he admitted. 'But I'm happy to know you're not planning to go anywhere.' He reached for the bill. 'And it didn't even take the promise of a pay rise to convince you to stay,' he mused. 'I'm proud of myself.'

Outside, he took her keys from her hand and unlocked her car; for a moment, while he was obviously inspecting the interior, Alisa was irritated at his nosiness. Then she realised that he was quietly making certain the car was empty before he allowed her to get in. The gentlemanly gesture might have been automatic—it was certainly the kind of caution that made sense in certain neighbourhoods of any city—but she decided she wasn't likely to come back to Emilio's alone.

'See you Monday,' he said, and started towards his car.

She lowered her window and called, 'I almost forgot. Happy birthday!'

He grimaced and came back to lean against her door. 'Don't remind me. As long as you're writing to Great-Aunt Louise, send that darned cheque back and tell her the best birthday gift I could get from her next year would be nothing. No card, no money—and no reminder that I'm getting older and I'm still not living up to her expectations.'

'I don't think she'd co-operate. After all, thirty-five isn't exactly antique compared to—how old is she, anyway? Eighty?'

'She's been a hundred and six ever since I've known her.'

'And, in any case, you can't hurt her feelings by sending her gift back. It just wouldn't be mannerly.'

He thought it over, and said slowly, 'All right. Tell her instead that I've spent the money on something I've wanted for a long time, and thank her effusively for making this the most wonderful birthday ever.'

'What are you going to buy?' Alisa asked, with foreboding.

He grinned, and under the dim street lights he looked about sixteen. 'A cellular telephone for my car. I'll call her up on it once, she'll never speak to me again, and that will solve all my problems!'

It was a long drive back across Phoenix to her apartment. It was a good thing that traffic was light, because she was too tired to pay proper attention to her driving, that was for sure. It had been a long and stressful week, and Justin Abernathy hadn't made it any better with his probing into her past.

Any normal person would have been looking forward to a quiet weekend, she thought, with the freedom to sleep late and laze around in pyjamas all day and eat junk food. But for Alisa the empty hours stretched out threateningly. If one couldn't sleep, and if doing nothing was not an appealing alternative, then a long weekend was nothing but an invitation to madness. A quiet apartment wasn't a sanctuary under those circumstances, but a cell. And the freedom to ignore the telephone wasn't liberty at all if the darned thing never rang—

The telephone. One good thing about that cross-examination over dinner, she reflected, was that for a while it had forced her to stop thinking about Shelley's call, and what it might mean. 'Things might change', Justin had said tonight. Was that what Shelley was calling about—to announce that she and Clay were splitting up? To cry on Alisa's shoulder?

Not likely, Alisa told herself. In any case, it didn't—couldn't—matter to her.

Or perhaps Shelley was calling to accuse her—

No, Alisa thought. Shelley had never known. Shelley must never know...

She was met at the door of her apartment by a Siamese cat who told her in no uncertain terms that she was sadly neglecting her duties. Once the thorough scolding was over, however, the cat graciously allowed himself to be picked up and cuddled, and he rewarded her with a steady, throaty puff. Alisa was in the kitchen trying to open a can of food for him while the animal rubbed his head against her hand and weaved himself back and forth through her arms, when the telephone rang beside her.

'Where have you been?' asked an unmistakable soft and breathless voice. 'I left a message for you hours ago. I suppose you've been out on a date.'

'Shelley, I tried to call. You didn't leave a number.'

There was an instant of silence, and then a laugh. 'I didn't? How utterly foolish of me. You've been calling all afternoon, and I haven't been home? You poor darling—I must have been delirious not to have thought of that.'

Alisa tightened her grip on the telephone. If the girl was here in the same room, she thought, I'd brain her with it. 'You did say it was urgent, Shelley,' she reminded. 'What is going on?'

'Oh, it is urgent—it's just the most wonderful news ever, that's all, and I've been going mad all afternoon waiting to tell you! I'm pregnant, darling. You're going to be an aunt next fall. Isn't it fantastic?'

Alisa groped for the back of a chair and sat down. My little sister is having a baby, she thought. Clay's baby. The baby that should have been mine.

She swallowed hard. 'How does Clay feel about it?'

'He's simply thrilled. You should see him; he sounds as if he's the one who invented babies. Aren't you happy for me?

You sound sort of—'

'Of course I'm delighted, Shelley. It's wonderful news.'

'And that's not all. I told Daddy I just had to see you, now—it's so important to me. And he gave us the plane tickets. Alisa, we'll be in Phoenix next Thursday, and we can stay two whole weeks!'

Alisa's hand was so tight on the telephone that cramps were shooting up her arm, but she couldn't make herself loosen her grip. The pain was the only thing that seemed quite real just now.

'Isn't it grand? We'll be able to stay up all night and eat and talk and giggle just like old times...'

'Just like old times'. For a moment the longing to have things back as they used to be—before Clay came into their lives—was so strong that it was like a plastic sheet draped over Alisa's head, suffocating her. If only, she thought, it were truly possible to go back to those days...

But there was no changing what had happened. She could not remake the past, she could only go forwards. And if that meant having Shelley—and Clay—here in Phoenix for two weeks, to face them every day, and have to hide her pain...

I can't do it, Alisa told herself. I can't stand it.

And yet, she's my sister, she thought. No matter what happened, that will always be the fact. I can't just refuse to let her come; I'd have to give some reason, and there is none, really, that wouldn't rouse everyone's suspicions. The truly important thing is that Shelley must never know about Clay and me. Especially now, with the baby coming. It would break her heart, and she's so happy.

And she is my sister...

'Of course you'll come,' Alisa said gently. 'I'll be waiting for you at the airport on Thursday.'

She put the telephone gently back in its cradle and buried her face in her hands.

Why didn't Clay stop her? she thought angrily. Why does he have to put me through this?

But she knew from experience that there really was no stopping Shelley, not once she had made up her mind. And as for Clay...

You shouldn't expect sensitivity from him, Alisa told herself. After all, the man eloped with your sister and didn't even tell you...

That isn't quite fair to Clay, she amended. He hadn't made me any promises, and so he didn't owe me any explanations. I was the one who saw commitment in every word, in every look. It wasn't his fault if I chose to fool myself.

But knowing that hadn't made the pain any easier to bear when he had married her sister instead. And running away hadn't eased the agony either, she admitted. Being half a continent away from the problem hadn't made the ache go away.

She raised her head, and dried her eyes, and squared her shoulders. The cat stared at her unblinkingly from the kitchen counter as she tidied up the mess from his meal, as if he could feel her pain. Her hands were shaking a little.

It will only be for two weeks, she

thought. Two weeks isn't long, really—only an eternity.

She took a deep breath. It might be good for me, too, she decided. It might be the best thing that could happen. Before a wound can heal, it must be cleansed. It hurts cruelly sometimes, but it has to be done.

Once she had faced the two of them, seen them together, forced herself to admit how happy they were—then, surely, she would be able to let go of the old pain and be content again, taking pleasure in her sister's joy?

She would make it happen that way. She had no other choice.

CHAPTER THREE

Alisa spent most of the weekend cleaning her apartment, making certain that every square inch had been vacuumed or dusted or scrubbed within an inch of its life. She didn't do it because the place was dirty, because it wasn't—she had always been a careful housekeeper—or because she thought Shelley would be critical. Mostly, she admitted to herself, she was cleaning because if she didn't do something she might just start screaming.

The cat didn't take kindly to the process; several times he rose from a comfortable perch when the vacuum cleaner approached, and stalked off with offended dignity to find another place to snooze. By early Sunday afternoon, when Alisa put the last of the cleaning supplies away, he had retreated to her bedroom, where he was curled up on her pillow with his paws over his eyes, as if denying that his comfortable world had come to this.

'This is what you get for complaining at me for being gone all the time,' Alisa told him as she retrieved her sandals from under the bed and her handbag from the wardrobe. 'Have a nice nap. I'm going to the supermarket.'

The cat sighed a little, as if in relief. Alisa laughed at him and went off in a brighter mood. At least talking to a pet wasn't likely to get her hauled off to a clinic for mental treatment, whereas talking to herself—

'The problem isn't that I talk to myself,' she concluded. 'It's all the thinking I'm doing—round and round like a hamster in an exercise wheel.' She hadn't slept much since Shelley had called. And if the forthcoming visit was bothering her so much already, how on earth was she going to get through two whole weeks of Shelley's company—and Clay's?

The only possible way, she knew, was to get her mind occupied with other things. That was why she stopped at the law office to pick up Louise Abernathy's letter. She might as well be thinking about the reply tonight, instead of worrying what next weekend would bring.

Normally Alisa made it a point not to go near the law office on weekends, but often on Monday mornings she knew from the stack of things on her desk that Justin had spent Sunday there. Nevertheless, she was startled when she found her door unlocked, and saw the lights on in his office.

Law books were piled unsteadily on the corner of his desk. One was open on the blotter, and Justin's elbows were propped on the desk, his hands supporting his head as he studied it.

'I didn't expect you to be here,' Alisa said from the doorway. 'I didn't see your car.'

He moved so suddenly that he nearly upset his office chair. 'So you came tiptoeing in to see who the burglar was? Sometimes you don't display a great deal of common sense, Mac.' He sounded grumpy.

It had obviously been quite a party last

71

night, she thought. 'I wasn't exactly trying to sneak in.'

He made a noise that might have been disagreement. 'Whether you were trying or not, you certainly succeeded.'

He leaned back in his chair and looked her over, and she immediately wished that she had put on something besides faded jeans that really were a little too tight. Then she decided that if he didn't like her attire it was his problem; what she wore outside working hours was not his concern.

'What are you doing here, anyway?' he asked.

'I came to get Louise's letter. I couldn't remember the details well enough to answer it.'

'Oh, yes.' He located the envelope under a stack of books and tossed it across the desk. 'As long as you're here,' he said, 'would you mind getting the Bartlett file out for me? I can't find it in that crazy filing system of yours to save my soul.'

'It's under "B",' she said gently. 'Are

you sure you should be trying to work today?'

'I wouldn't be here at all if it weren't for that damned recorder the other day—plus the fact that I forgot to take one home with me. Thank you,' he added with strict politeness, as she handed him the folder.

'I thought perhaps, under the circumstances—'

'Under what circumstances?'

'Well, with your birthday party last night and everything—you're obviously not feeling well.'

He slammed the folder down on the desk. 'That does it! So you're the one who's to blame for this! I want an explanation, Mac. What in hell made you tell Debbie that yesterday was my birthday?'

Alisa blinked in utter shock at the attack. 'I didn't,' she croaked. 'She already knew.'

Justin looked as if he didn't believe her. 'How did she find out?'

'How would I know? I certainly didn't tell her—I didn't know it myself till Louise's card came in Friday's mail.'

He stared at her for a long moment. 'Nobody could have put that abominable party together in a single day, that's true.' He sounded reluctant to admit the possibility.

'Well, maybe she went to the newspaper office and looked up your files in the morgue.'

'She's lucky she isn't in the morgue this morning.'

'It was that bad, hmm?' Alisa sat down on the corner of his desk. 'Didn't you enjoy being the guest of honour? Or is it just the hangover that's bothering you?'

'I do not have a hangover!'

'Oh? You imitate it rather well.'

'The woman had a hundred people there doing idiotic things like playing spin the bottle and pin the tail on the donkey, celebrating the last wave of my lost youth. I hate that sort of stupid celebration, and then when you add to it that I didn't know it was coming—'

'I see that you didn't enjoy it,' Alisa murmured.

'You could have warned me, Mac.

Obviously you knew about it—'

'And spoil the surprise? How was I to know you hated things like that? Besides, she only told me on Friday.'

'I had no idea you and Debbie were such close friends. Sharing all your girlhood secrets—'

'Didn't you?' Alisa asked airily. 'I'd have thought, when she promised to introduce me to her ex, that it was obvious—'

He had stopped listening. 'The re-creation of the childhood party was bad enough,' he said, 'with the crêpe paper streamers and the helium balloons and all. But then when people got bored with that and started getting drunk and falling in the pool...'

It was all Alisa could do to keep from laughing. 'It sounds unique,' she said soberly. 'I think you should be thrilled that she cared enough to go to all that trouble.'

He growled. If she didn't know better, Alisa would have thought he was pretending to be a grizzly bear at the zoo. She slid off the desk and tiptoed towards the door, keeping one eye on him.

'Mac, do you promise on your honour that if you ever get wind of another surprise party you will tell me instantly?'

She eyed him warily. 'The ethical implications of that question require considerable thought—'

He pushed his chair back and started towards her with determination.

'But now that I've had a chance to think it over,' she added, very quickly, 'yes, I'll tell you. Instantly. Even before that, truly—'

He began to laugh. 'Oh, for heaven's sake, Mac, don't run away. I'm not going to get out my Swiss army knife and carve you into slices.'

'You aren't?' She heaved a theatrical sigh of relief. 'Still, I think I'll get out of here while it's safe.'

She was almost to the door when he called, 'Would you turn the copy machine on for me?'

She did, and then came back to the door of his office. 'Have you ever run that thing?' She idly picked up his broken tape recorder from the shelf of the bookcase, took the batteries out, put them back in right side up, and pressed the button. It worked.

'No. What's the problem? You put the original in and push the button and presto! You get five hundred duplicates.'

She looked at him for a long time. The photocopier was the most updated version produced by the premier company in the business, and it had been installed just two weeks ago. It resembled a small printing press rather than a regular copier; it was half the size of a car, and it had more controls than the average aircraft. It had taken her two days to figure out the finer details of operating it. Turning Justin Abernathy loose with it would be an invitation to disaster.

With his lack of mechanical co-ordination, she thought, he'd be apt to fall into the machine and duplicate himself, and then I'd have five hundred of him to cope with...

She put the recorder back on his desk and tossed her handbag into a chair. 'Just let me know what you need. I'll make the copies.'

'I thought you were in a hurry.'

'It can wait,' she said crisply.

It was a couple of hours later that she put the last stack of pages on his desk. He smiled absently, rubbed the back of his neck and said, 'You're a gem, Mac. I'm truly sorry to destroy your peaceful Sunday afternoon.'

She didn't tell him that it wouldn't have been very peaceful if she'd gone home and spent the time wondering what mechanical nightmares would be waiting for her at the office in the morning. 'I was just going to the supermarket, actually,' she said. 'I can do that any time.'

He looked interested. 'The cat ate the rest of the tuna?'

'No—I'm having guests for a couple of weeks.'

'Friends from home?'

'My sister and her husband.' This could be slippery territory, she thought, and added, 'Their timing is awful, I'm afraid. Can I take a long lunch-hour on Thursday to meet their plane?'

His eyes narrowed. 'Sometimes I don't believe you're real, Mac. If you kept track of the extra time you spend here, you could have a long lunch-hour every day—and probably a week's vacation left over at the end of the year. Take the day off. I'd give you the whole two weeks, but there is such a thing as keeping the office running.'

The mere idea gave her the shivers. 'I wouldn't dream of taking extra time off,' she said firmly. 'It was a last-minute decision to come, you see, and they're not expecting me to entertain them every minute.'

'Still, it isn't every day you have company.'

And we should all be humbly grateful for that, Alisa thought.

'So you're going to the supermarket to stock up, hmm? Do you like to cook, Mac?'

'Now and then. It's more fun when there's a crowd.' Or one enthusiastic eater, she thought. Clay had always enjoyed his food...

Stop it, she told herself. That's the past, and you aren't going to waste today thinking about it.

Justin looked thoughtful. 'In that case, maybe you could help me,' he said, sounding almost a little hesitant. 'If you wouldn't mind my tagging along, that is. My problem is that I never know what to buy, and so I stay miles from supermarkets and end up eating out instead. If I just knew...'

He didn't use the million-watt smile; she had been prepared for that. It was the wistful look in his eyes that disarmed her. And, after all, the man had just offered her an extra day off...

That was why she ended up wheeling a trolley through Smitty's, elbow-to-elbow with Justin Abernathy, giving him a brief home economics lesson at every turn of the aisle, selecting the freshest chicken breasts and vegetables, and instructing him on how to cook a stir-fry.

In the car park, after the bags were loaded into their cars, he said, 'Thanks, Mac. I only hope I can remember how to do all that. Was it the green pepper that went in first, or the mushrooms?'

She swore under her breath. 'Neither. It was—oh, come on over. I'll show you how to do it, and write it down for you.'

He rewarded her with a smile. 'It's awfully nice of you.'

She got into her car and slammed the door. It wasn't until she was halfway to her apartment that she realised she hadn't given him the address. But the red Cadillac pulled into the apartment complex right behind her, and Justin leaned out.

'I've been thinking,' he announced. 'Won't it be a hassle to take all my extra stuff in, and then haul it all out again? And I shouldn't just leave it in the car for an hour or two, should I?'

Alisa closed her eyes and thought about the contents of those bags—ice-cream, frozen vegetables, meat. 'No, it wouldn't be a good idea to leave it in the car,' she said with commendable restraint.

'Then why don't we unload your stuff, and take mine out to my house? That way we only have to do things once—it's more efficient. Besides, if you demonstrate in my kitchen I'll know which pans to use and everything.'

It made perfect sense, actually, and the fact that she couldn't pick a flaw in his logic irritated her. 'You honestly own pans?' Alisa asked. She fished her apartment key out of the bottom of her handbag and picked up an armful of groceries.

'The first housekeeper bought some.' He carried up the rest of the food and then shadow-boxed with the cat while she unpacked the bags. 'This is a beautiful animal, Mac.'

'And spoilt, too. Half the time I call him The Brat. He's an annoyance sometimes, but having an animal around makes it much harder to take life too seriously.'

'What's his name, really?'

'Vibrato—if he stops playing and starts to purr you'll see why. The entire apartment sort of hums along with him.'

He looked around, and Alisa appreciated his tact when he didn't say anything. Her surroundings weren't the most elegant;

she had put most of her own furniture into storage in Green Bay and taken a year's lease on this furnished apartment. When the year was up, she had already decided, she would find a place that was more to her taste—something that didn't reverberate like a kettledrum every time a neighbour slammed a door—and have her own things shipped down. In the meantime, a few personal touches made a lot of difference—a couple of needlepoint cushions on the couch, and her favourite prints on the walls, and her house plants everywhere.

'It's not very big, is it?' he said. 'You'll have cramped quarters for a couple of weeks with two more people here.'

I know, Alisa thought. We'll be tripping over each other all the time. But there was no easy way to suggest that Shelley and Clay might be more comfortable staying in a hotel instead. In any case, Alisa certainly couldn't afford to pay the rates at this season, and Shelley would see no reason to, when her sister had an extra bedroom...

'We'll manage,' she said, and didn't realise how short-tempered she sounded until she saw Justin's eyebrows go up.

He didn't say anything more, just walked across the tiny dining area to look out of the glass doors at the minuscule covered terrace. 'That's not patio furniture, is it?'

'The fern stand I'm refinishing?'

'Is that what it is?'

'Yes—Vibrato thinks my Boston fern is a salad, so I'm going to put it on the stand where he can't reach it. It's on the patio because it smells too bad most of the time to bring it inside.'

'You just leave it out there?'

She nodded. 'The place is well guarded —that's one advantage of living here.'

'You make it sound as if there aren't many.'

'Well—' She realised abruptly that he sounded serious, and stopped. Why point out the defects if he hadn't seen them for himself? She finished putting the groceries away in a thoughtful silence.

Outside, she started to unlock her car and said, over her shoulder, 'I'll have to stop for gas. It's quite a way out to your house, isn't it?'

'Don't bother. I'll bring you back. Besides, you haven't seen my new toy yet.' He helped her into the Cadillac and walked around to slide behind the wheel.

'The phone,' she said. 'You've got it already?'

'Sure. They put it in yesterday.' He started the engine and waited till the convertible's top folded neatly back.

'Then you can't have done it just because of your great-aunt Louise.'

'Do you promise not to tell her? You're right; I'd been thinking about it for a while. I really wished that I'd had it on Friday. Then I could just have called you up and dictated all the way back from Flagstaff and not bothered with that silly recorder.' He looked quite pleased with himself.

'What a lovely idea,' Alisa said faintly.

His house lay to the north of Phoenix proper, in a fairly new development at the foot of one of the small, rugged mountains that surrounded the Valley of the Sun. He didn't slow down at the small building that marked the entrance, merely waved at a uniformed guard standing nearby. The man made a frantic gesture, and the Cadillac screeched to a halt a few feet further on.

'A package came for you this afternoon, Mr Abernathy,' the guard said. 'Mrs Baxter dropped it off.' He darted a glance at Alisa, as if gauging her reaction to the news that she was not the only woman in Justin Abernathy's life. She wanted to shrink down into her seat and disappear; it certainly didn't take much intuition to know what the guard was thinking.

Justin glanced at the package. It was wrapped in red foil with a silver bow. 'In case she comes back, Roger,' he said, 'remember—you haven't seen me all day.' He threw the package over his shoulder into the back of the car.

The guard grinned. 'You've got it, Mr Abernathy.' He grinned at Alisa and half saluted as the Cadillac pulled away.

Alisa said pointedly, 'You could hardly have picked up the package if you haven't been anywhere near the place. If she were to have second thoughts and ask for it back—' But just then the Cadillac turned into a driveway, and she got her first good look at his house.

She didn't quite know what she had been expecting, but it wasn't this sprawling, adobe-coloured structure, surrounded by a high, thick wall interrupted at regular intervals by lacy wrought-iron panels. Inside the wall lay a flagstone courtyard with a fountain in the centre. Nearer the house was a neat arrangement of yukka plants and a huge saguaro cactus, stretching its long arms in supplication towards the sky. And over the peaked red-tile roof of the central portion of the house she caught a glimpse of something that looked like a palm tree.

This isn't a house, she thought, it's an estate.

'Inside the city limits,' she said, 'they'd call this a resort, and they'd build thirty town houses and a pool.'

Justin laughed. 'It's got the pool, at least.' There was a garage, too, but he parked the car just outside it and started to gather up bags.

Alisa picked up the red-foil package.

'Just leave it there,' he said easily. 'If it explodes, it'll do less damage here than inside.'

She put it down gingerly. 'In that case, I'm surprised you didn't leave it at the guard shack.'

He looked surprised. 'Roger's a nice guy. I wouldn't want him to get hurt.'

Alisa nodded. 'Of course. It's obvious that you told Debbie you weren't wild about the surprise party.'

'I think I made myself clear, yes.'

'It's probably an apology,' she suggested. 'A bottle of wine, I'd say, from the shape.'

Justin shrugged. 'Or a Molotov cocktail. She was pretty hot under the collar. Open it if you like, and we'll see.'

'You don't want Roger to get hurt, but it's all right if it explodes in my face—is that it?'

He laughed. 'Mac, you know I can't do without you. Now that I think about it, it probably isn't explosive after all. If she didn't get mad enough to firebomb me during her divorce, I guess she wouldn't be likely to now. Open it—if you're right, we'll drink it with dinner.'

'Thanks anyway,' Alisa said. 'But I think I'll stay out of it, just in case she put a little arsenic in the bottle. I'm really just an innocent bystander, like Roger.'

His kitchen looked forlornly unused. It looked as if every appliance known to mankind had been installed, and then promptly forgotten. The expensive electric range was as spotlessly clean as the day it had been manufactured. The open bookshelves above a small desk in one corner were bare. One of the housekeepers, no doubt, had been responsible for the set of heavy glass canisters that were neatly lined up on one broad counter; they, too, were empty, and somehow, Alisa thought, that was the saddest-looking part of all. It was a kitchen any gourmet cook would kill for, and it had obviously never been used.

He opened a cabinet door with a flourish.

'Pans,' he announced. 'Anything you need, I should think.'

'Well, find a nice skillet and wash your hands and get that chicken out of the bag—'

'I thought you were going to show me how.'

'I'll tell you what to do, but the best way to learn is to do it yourself.' She said it very soberly, and she was a bit surprised to catch a fleeting look of astonishment on his face.

Why did he think I agreed to come out here, anyway? she wondered with a tinge of anger. I came to give him a cooking lesson; surely he doesn't think it's a different twist on the old 'Come up and see my etchings' line...?

But the astonishment was gone so quickly that she found herself wondering if she had really seen it at all. And he certainly pitched into the food with a will, chopping onions with an enthusiasm that threatened to have them both in tears within minutes.

Cleaning up, she thought, might have to

be a lesson all by itself—but it probably won't be taught by me.

'What a wonderful kitchen,' she said, as she folded the last empty bag and stored it neatly under the sink.

'It is?' He sounded genuinely interested in her opinion. 'I always thought it was too big—it's miles between things. And as for all these useless gadgets...'

Alisa stopped and stared at him. 'If you don't have any idea what everything is for, then why did you put it all in?'

'I didn't. It was already here when I moved in. I bought the house from the Andersons—you remember them? They had the especially nasty custody battle.'

She nodded. 'He lived in the recreational vehicle in their driveway for months while they argued about who got the kids.'

'This very driveway,' Justin agreed.

'And she kept unplugging his electrical supply, till you told her that if she did it one more time the judge was going to hold her in contempt of court. I remember. What I don't understand is why you bought a house with a kitchen like this.

If you don't even know what most of the appliances are for—'

'It was one way to be sure the Andersons had enough money to pay my fees,' he said earnestly.

She laughed, despite herself. She certainly didn't believe him, but she had to admit that the man had a knack for avoiding questions he didn't want to answer.

'I think a fire might be nice,' Justin said.

'And you're going to have one any minute if you don't turn the heat down under that skillet.'

'No, I meant in the living-room, so we can eat beside it. I'll go and light it—'

'And then disappear while I finish dinner? You're not getting out of it that easily. Point me in the right direction, and I'll take care of the fire.'

'You can?'

'You ask that of a Wisconsin girl? I've been playing with fire since I was a Brownie scout.'

He looked a little doubtful, but he didn't

argue. 'The living-room is through there and sort of around the bend.'

He wasn't exaggerating; the bend took her through a long, narrow butler's pantry with enough cabinets to store china for a hundred, and then through a large dining-room—at least, Alisa thought, it would have been a dining-room if it had been furnished. As it was, the low-hanging brass and crystal chandelier looked severely out of place in the empty room. It certainly explained why Justin hadn't suggested having dinner there.

She pushed open a set of double doors and stepped into the living-room, and almost cried out in surprise.

It was a long, airy room, open all the way to the peaked roof line, with huge, age-darkened beams spanning the width of the room at the place where an ordinary house would have had a ceiling. Those beams hadn't come from anywhere local, Alisa thought, and it must have cost a fortune to ship them in. The fireplace mantel centred on the long front wall was enormous and ornately carved and obviously just as old as the beams. Possibly French, she thought.

The room occupied almost the entire width of this central section of the house; tall windows on either side of the fireplace looked out on to the courtyard, and at the back a long, narrow sun-porch ran the length of the living-room, with the pool lying beyond. Under the last rays of sunlight, the water looked like hammered gold.

At the other end of the living-room there was another set of double doors; they were closed, but they must lead to the bedroom wing, she concluded. The house was even larger than it had looked from outside. What was it he had said, about buying it so he didn't have to worry about clutter? It had to be huge, she thought, because there wasn't any clutter in the living-room yet. In fact, there was scarcely anything at all, and certainly not much that could be called furniture. The only place to sit was a love-seat that matched the curtains.

'And that explains why it's here,' Alisa murmured. Her voice sounded loud in

94

the almost empty room. 'The Andersons must have left the stuff that matched the house.'

And yet, despite the slightly dusty emptiness, it was a pleasant room, one that invited a person to curl up on that love-seat with a glass of wine and a good book, beside a crackling fire...

That reminded her of why she was here. Beside the fireplace was a brass log-holder and a basket full of kindling, and in a couple of minutes she had a pleasant little blaze started. The evening was going to be just cool enough for the heat to be welcome, and flames licking at a log had always been one of Alisa's favourite sights. She was tempted to stay in this peaceful room and just watch the fire, but conscience drew her back to the kitchen to keep a careful eye on her pupil. Conscience and, she had to admit, hunger.

The stir-fry turned out very well, all things considered. They had a sort of picnic in front of the fire, and she complimented Justin on the outcome of the experiment. He shrugged and said, 'Don't give me too much credit. I probably couldn't do it again without a coach.'

'I'll write it all down for you.'

He brought her a snifter of brandy and settled himself on the hearthrug again.

She stretched out on her side, propping herself up on her elbow, and stared at the fire, letting the brandy warm against her palm. Then she sipped it and sighed. 'Wonderful,' she said. 'Take my advice, Justin, and choose your interior decorator carefully.'

He shuddered. 'What's wrong with leaving it the way it is?'

She sat up. 'There is a happy medium between a furniture showroom and an abandoned warehouse,' she pointed out.

He looked around. 'I guess it does look a little empty,' he conceded handsomely.

'But don't let the decorator fill up every nook, either. You're very lucky, you know, to have all this sheer space. To say nothing of luxuries like the pool. My next apartment is going to have a pool,' she added dreamily. 'Of course, some day when I have a house—' She stopped abruptly. When she was tired, or relaxed, or otherwise off guard, her version of 'some day' still included Clay. And that, right now, was downright dangerous.

'What's wrong with the apartment you've got? It certainly looked comfortable.'

He was completely serious, she saw. Obviously what he had seen at her apartment hadn't been the quality of the furniture, but the atmosphere she had tried to create. All those homey little touches had had the desired effect after all, she thought. 'Oh, it's just that some day I'd like to have a place that's really mine—so I can paint the walls purple if I liked. Not that I'd actually do it,' she added hastily. 'It's really that I hate having to ask someone's permission before I do something simple like put up a bookshelf or hang a window-shade.'

'I know. That's why I bought the house.' He grinned lazily. 'That, and also because I want to take pictures of it back to my law-school reunion this summer, and show them what a success I am.'

She didn't believe that for a minute; if he honestly felt the need to prove himself by displaying material success, he would also have been showing off to his Phoenix friends. He would have hired a decorator the instant he'd bought the house, and he'd be having parties every weekend to display his prize. No, she thought, if there is one thing Justin Abernathy isn't, it's a braggart.

'I'll write you a testimonial if you like,' Alisa offered gently. 'I'm sure all your former classmates would like to know that the first issue to be negotiated in a Phoenix divorce isn't temporary alimony and child support, it's which spouse gets you to represent them.'

'That's very generous of you, Mac. But that won't be necessary.'

She smothered a small smile. She'd been right; she had called his bluff, and he had promptly backed down.

He poked at the fire and said thoughtfully, 'I'll probably just let my wife tell them how wonderful I am.'

Alisa choked on her brandy.

He added kindly, 'Does that startle you, Mac? It shouldn't. I've decided to get married, that's all—not commit murder.'

CHAPTER FOUR

Alisa wasn't just startled; she was nearly overwhelmed by shock. It took her a full minute to stop coughing, and even then she couldn't quite get her breathing back to normal.

Justin was watching her with rapt interest.

'I'm stunned,' she said honestly. 'Aren't you the one who said Adam should have used the fig-leaf to draw up a pre-nuptial contract to protect his rights to the Garden of Eden?'

'I dare say I am—then it wouldn't have been considered community property. But I certainly never said that I don't believe in marriage.' He sounded a bit testy. 'I just think most people go about it all wrong.'

'Oh? And you've got the right way figured out?' She tried to fight off the desire to laugh; something told her this

100

was not the time to succumb to giggles. 'Well, I'm glad to hear that. And I'm very grateful that you let me know before any formal announcement was made. But don't you think you could have told me at the office just as well? Most women would have a fit at the idea of your breaking the news to your secretary in surroundings like this, you know.' She waved her brandy glass in a gesture that encompassed the room, the fire, the remains of their intimate dinner. 'Your fiancée must be very—understanding.'

He swirled the brandy in his glass and drained it. 'I don't have one, actually.'

'One what?' Alisa asked, honestly at a loss for an instant.

'Fiancée.'

She stared at him. 'Now, wait a minute. How can you be getting married if you don't have a fiancée?'

'I mean I don't have one yet. I haven't exactly decided who to marry, just that—'

She couldn't help it. She rolled on to her back, screaming with laughter, holding her sides and howling.

Justin frowned. He tapped his foot against the stone hearth with an air of long-suffering patience, until Alisa finally sat up and wiped her eyes with her napkin. 'Sorry,' she said unrepentantly. 'But if this isn't the craziest thing I've ever heard, it's close.'

'What's crazy about it? Getting married is a very sensible thing to do.'

'I'm not sure that "sensible" is quite the right—' She saw the annoyed light in his eyes, swallowed the rest of the sentence, and added diplomatically, 'Why don't you tell me what prompted this decision?'

'It seems to be the right time,' he said, a little stiffly. 'I've established myself in my profession now, so I'm financially secure and able to provide for a wife. And, much as I hate to admit it, I am thirty-five, so if I'm going to have a family I shouldn't wait too long.'

'Oh, a family, too,' Alisa said, on a note of discovery. 'Tell me, did you plan all this out on your life's calendar long ago? "Graduate from law school, establish practice, buy convertible, turn thirty-five, get married, have one point eight children—"?'

'What is wrong with planning ahead?'

She ignored the interruption. 'Your priorities are interesting, to say the least. Didn't you overlook something? What happened to falling in love?'

'Falling in love is where the trouble usually starts,' he said dogmatically. 'Every couple who ends up in my office to file a divorce action thought they were in love. Love is a charming, romantic concept that causes all sorts of grief in the world, because when love comes in the window practical concerns go straight out of the door. All those couples in love didn't give a thought to the logical, sensible problems of living together. I saw one marriage actually break up because he liked to go deer hunting and she thought blood sports were horrifying, but they had never considered that little disagreement before they married, because they were in love.' He rolled his eyes and said, with a saccharine overtone, 'Surely you know, my dear, that *true love* will solve *everything.*'

Alisa had to smile at his vicious mimicry of romantic sentimentalism, but her voice was serious. 'You can't believe that being in love dooms a marriage, Justin—'

'No. Sometimes the partners in a marriage are lucky, and when they fall out of love—'

'You say that as if it's inevitable!'

'It certainly is. Nobody can live at that peak forever—it's exhausting and unrealistic. When they fall out of love, a lot of partners find they can't stand each other and call it quits. But a few lucky ones discover that they were accidentally well matched in spite of themselves, and they get to be friends, which is a lot more long-lasting anyway.'

Alisa shook her head. 'What a perfectly cold-blooded—'

'There's nothing cold-blooded about it. I'm just bypassing the nonsense and eliminating all the risk-taking. I'm not surprised that you're letting this upset you, Mac—but I'm sure that once you really understand the concept, you'll agree that it's by far the most sensible approach.'

'I wouldn't put any money on it.'

'Let's take you and your true love, for example.'

'Let's not.' It was flat and firm.

He looked startled, but he said, agreeably enough, 'All right, then, let's take me. Let's say, for the sake of argument, that I had fallen head over heels in love with Debbie Baxter, and married her. And last night I came home from a tough week's work to be greeted with a surprise party. Certainly it's not a major problem, but, believe me, it would be enough to put an end to the fiction of love; I've seen sillier things bring a screeching halt to—'

'I'll remember to write that into your pre-nuptial contract, if you find anyone crazy enough to agree to this proposition,' Alisa murmured. 'Surprise parties shall be considered grounds for divorce.'

'No divorce. Dammit, don't you understand what I'm saying at all, Mac? I'm going to do this once, and I'm going to do it right. I absolutely refuse to mess up my life with a divorce—I refuse to quarrel over alimony and child support and custody.'

'You can't do that,' she protested. 'You can't just announce, "There will be no divorce!" as if it's a royal edict, you know. What are you going to do if she changes her mind—lock her in a dungeon somewhere?'

'It's not a threat, Mac, it's more of a guarantee. Once that commitment is made, there will be no looking back, no reason to ask if it was the right thing to do, and no wondering if there's something better out there. It worked for centuries before there was such a thing as easy divorce, you know. People got married for life, and, no matter what happened, they worked things out—'

'And some of them were miserable.'

'But most of them weren't. The best way to avoid problems is to make sure there aren't any false expectations from the beginning. Love is a false expectation by definition, because it can't last forever. I'd rather have an honest bargain. No,' he added thoughtfully, 'a partnership—that's a better way to put it—with benefits to both sides. I'm going to find a logical, sensible woman who agrees with me—'

'Where?' Alisa interrupted. 'Are you going to run an ad in the Personals column, or go on national television?'

'Well, I'll tell you where I'm not looking. I'm not interested in one of the bored society girls who is always finding a new game to entertain herself with—'

'This will break Debbie Baxter's heart, you know. After she invested in the bottle of wine and everything—'

'Because women who are bored by their lives now would soon be bored with marriage too, and looking for a new source of entertainment.'

'Don't you think you're underestimating yourself, Justin?' It was a wicked murmur.

'I'm looking for someone who will appreciate what I'm offering—'

'I'm sure they'll be standing in line.'

He sent a sharp glance at her, and then went on, seriously. 'I'm prepared to be generous—I can afford to be.'

'Don't you think it would be cheaper just to hire another housekeeper?'

'Mac, you're deliberately misunderstanding me. I don't want a housekeeper!'

'I stand corrected. You're looking for a robot—logical, reasonable, and feeling no emotion. I'm glad you told me all this before I answered Louise's letter—I'd have felt a complete fool if I'd explained why you weren't getting married, and next week I had to take it all back. I can't wait to tell her—she'll be so thrilled at the news.'

'I know,' he said morosely. 'That's the one drawback to it—Great-Aunt Louise will take all the credit.'

'Then perhaps you should think better of it,' Alisa suggested gently.

'No.' He sounded determined. 'I've ignored her advice for ten years and been very happy with myself, but things have changed; it would be foolish to refuse to do what I want just in order to spite her.'

Alisa shook her head a little. 'I still can't believe I'm hearing correctly, you know,' she said finally. 'Honestly, Justin, I know you've seen a lot of stupidity in the divorces you've handled, but that's hardly a fair survey! To conclude from what you see in your office that there's no such thing as love—'

'Oh, I think there's a kind of love that develops sometimes. But as for romantic love—what so many people call "true love", in that syrupy tone of voice—I don't believe in it, no. It's a figment of the imagination.' He frowned. 'No, not imagination. Actually, I think it's a case of hormones running wild.'

'I'm so glad you clarified that,' Alisa said with soft sarcasm. 'I find it reassuring.'

He poked at the fire and put another small log on. 'You see, romantic love is a concept that has no history and no real validity. It's an invention of, the western world, and most of the rest of the globe finds the whole idea ludicrous. Even in the west, it was scarcely heard of a couple of centuries ago—'

'Thanks for the history lesson. Do you actually think we should go back to arranged marriages?'

'They were certainly successful in keeping the world going, weren't they? We didn't have any shortage of new people, and society was a whole lot more stable.'

'That's an entirely different thing. You can't give credit for everything good about the world to the custom of arranging marriages.'

'All right, I won't. But what was so wrong with it?'

'If you think it's so wonderful, why don't you ask your Great-Aunt Louise if she has a girl in mind for you?'

'There are limits, Mac.'

'Then you're not really serious about it. If you insist on choosing this lucky woman for yourself, the one who is perfect for your plans, aren't you really saying that—'

'That's not it at all. You see, romance says that there is one man for every woman, one woman for every man, and you shall know your one perfect love by the way your hormone levels jump when you meet that ideal person.'

'Really, Justin, don't you think that's putting it just a little strongly?'

'Not at all. I think the idea of romance—the gospel of one perfect love—is nonsense. For any one person there are a hundred compatible marriages, if he or she is willing to keep an open mind and not let the glands have more to say about it than the brain does. Instead, people insist on thinking that if they can't have that one perfect person, nothing else is worth considering. Like you, when your one perfect love dumped you—'

She said crisply, to side-track that line of observation, 'So you believe that sexual attraction isn't important?'

'I didn't say that, Mac. But it certainly isn't the only thing that matters. Some day a man has to get out of bed and turn on the lights—and what if he doesn't like the woman he sees? What if he doesn't want to spend his days with her, as well as his nights?'

'I can't wait to see the faces of these hopeful women when you ask them to fill out an application form listing their hobbies and interests!'

The sarcasm seemed to bounce off him. 'I don't think it needs to be that complicated, Ailsa.'

'Oh? I suppose you want me to interview them instead?'

'No.' He stretched himself out more comfortably, clasped his hands at the back of his neck, and stared into the fire. 'I think you should marry me yourself.'

This time she didn't feel like laughing. 'And I think that you—' she began furiously, and then thought better of it. He might have suddenly turned into a madman, but he was still her boss, and that called for tactful handling of this unsuspected obsession. To say nothing of the purely practical matter that at the moment she was miles and miles out in the desert, with no car.

'I think I'd like another brandy,' she said finally.

He picked up her glass and crossed the room to the little bar hidden in a corner cabinet. While his back was turned, Alisa concentrated on taking deep breaths, and by the time he returned she was fairly calm again. She took the snifter, swallowed a mouthful of brandy that she didn't want, and said, 'May I ask how many women

112

have turned you down already?'

He looked surprised. 'None. Why?'

'Well, I'm flattered that you've given me first refusal, but—'

'You shouldn't be,' he said in a matter-of-fact tone. He stretched out beside her. 'You're intelligent, organised, willing to compromise. Those are all traits that are necessary to make a successful marriage. You're also a hard worker—you've supported yourself and so I'm confident you won't fling away carelessly what I've worked hard to build. And—'

'Thank you,' she said firmly. What a catalogue of virtues to accompany a proposal! Hysteria was rising inside her, along with an overwhelming need to take control of the conversation before it slid any further into surrealism. 'I'm very grateful for the compliment, you understand,' she said, and crossed her fingers firmly behind her back at the white lie. 'But it's really impossible. I simply couldn't—'

'Why not? I think it's ideal. Where else are you going to find a man who thinks it's a terrific idea to have a bunch of kids and a wife who stays at home with them? You told me yourself that that was your dream. Face it, Alisa—men like that are an endangered species these days. Even if they can afford it, a lot of them don't want the responsibility. I think it's a neat idea—'

'I'm not looking for a man,' she began stiffly.

'Not at all? Not ever? How old are you, Alisa?'

She couldn't think of a reason not to tell him. 'I'm twenty-six.'

'You could be alone for sixty years. That's a long time to mourn for your true love.'

It wasn't fair, she thought; he had put her on the defensive, and he had done it so smoothly that she couldn't even find the seam in his logic.

'That's one of the reasons I made you the offer,' he went on. 'You've found out for yourself that romantic love doesn't work. That's the biggest thing that concerns me about this plan, you know—that a woman might agree with the idea, but still think, subconsciously, that I'll change my mind some day. It would be pretty uncomfortable to have a wife who was cherishing hopes like that.'

'Well, I certainly don't,' Alisa said tartly.

He smiled approvingly. 'I know. All your little romantic notions were forcibly removed long ago. It's too bad that you got hurt, of course, but in the long run it's really very lucky. Now you can be realistic about things, and there is no reason why we couldn't be quite reasonably contented together.'

That, she thought, was the most hard-hearted thing she had ever heard anyone say. To tell her that losing Clay was the luckiest thing that had ever happened to her, and to reduce the hope of marital happiness that every woman cherished to a matter of 'reasonable contentment'—as if he was suggesting something no more important than an evening out...

'No, thank you,' she said firmly. 'It's not because of—' she caught herself just before Clay's name slipped out, and went on '—the man I loved, either. But there are other things that are more important to me than money and material possessions, or even than children would be. I might never have children, but I will have my self-respect.'

'Self-respect is fine, Mac, but I've found that a righteous attitude isn't a lot of comfort on a cold night.'

Before she could start to scream, he shrugged his shoulders and smiled. 'But it's up to you, of course. No hard feelings.'

He doused the fire, and on the way back to Phoenix he kept the conversation firmly on ordinary matters—the cases that would need attention through the week, the forthcoming court calendar. Gradually Alisa relaxed, and just as they reached her apartment complex she said, with a wry smile, 'See? You don't really want to marry me, Justin. I'm too valuable in the office.'

'That would have been a problem,' he agreed. He parked the Cadillac and turned to face her, his elbow propped against the leather back of the bucket seat. 'But thanks for considering it, at least. I hope you don't take it personally, Mac—I mean, I am still going to marry someone, so...'

Alisa laughed, a little nervously. 'And you're hoping that I'll never tell your wife that you proposed to me first? You don't need to worry about that.' Though as a matter of fact, she thought, the sort of logical, practical female he was looking for probably wouldn't be disturbed at all by the news!

He smiled. 'In that case, there is one more thing—just to satisfy my curiosity.' His hand slipped to the back of her neck, and he leaned towards her.

In the confined space of the bucket seat, with her seat-belt still fastened, there was nowhere for Alisa to go. She made a little noise of protest, which he ignored, and then she could do nothing more, for his mouth had found hers.

Don't be a fool, she told herself. It's only a kiss. Don't make a scene about it.

It was a very pleasant caress, soft, gentle, easy—as casual as if he were sampling a new flavour of ice-cream, Alisa thought. When he raised his head, finally, she said,

'Well? Is your curiosity satisfied?' She was proud of her tone of voice; she sounded amused, cheerful—precisely as she had wanted to do.

He smiled. 'Oh, yes. See you tomorrow, Mac.'

She stumbled up to her apartment, grateful for the quiet darkness. 'As if I would tell anyone about that insane proposition,' she said to the Siamese cat when he came to rub himself against her ankles. 'Certainly not his wife—when and if he ever finds one. Who would believe me if I repeated that pack of nonsense, anyway? As a matter of fact, the best thing I could do is to forget this entire crazy day as soon as I possibly can.'

If I'm lucky, she thought, it will only take me a year or two.

She had prepared herself for a bit of uneasiness at the office, but days went by and the subject did not come up again. Justin was quite his ordinary self, demanding and disarming by turns; the workload was heavier than usual because of his absence the week before, and Alisa was beginning to wonder if the whole thing had been nothing more than her own fevered nightmare. Had she really sat on the floor of Justin's living-room and listened to that incredible line of reasoning? One of them had gone completely berserk, she was sure; she just wasn't certain which one it had been.

On Thursday morning Ridge Coltrain brought the Goulds' tentative property settlement back in tatters; Mr Gould, it seemed, had some definite ideas about the things he would not give up. Justin ushered his young opponent into his office and said over his shoulder, 'We may be a couple of hours hashing this out, Mac, but we're going to get it done. Will you make a lunch reservation for us? We'll either be still negotiating, or celebrating, but we'll have to eat.'

'Make it for three,' Ridge Coltrain suggested, 'and come along.' He grinned at Justin. 'I have a feeling I might be able to negotiate faster if I can look forward to a non-business lunch with Alisa.'

Alisa shook her head. 'Sorry to disappoint you, Ridge, but I have to meet a plane.'

Justin's eyes narrowed. 'I'd forgotten. You were going to take the day off.'

'No—I told you I just needed a long lunch-hour.'

He looked at her thoughtfully for a long moment. 'Pardon me while I deal with a personnel problem, Ridge,' he said.

Ridge Coltrain smiled. 'If he fires you, Alisa, remember that—' he began, just as Justin closed the office door and shut him off.

'Mac,' he said gently, 'you haven't had a day off in months. As much as I appreciate your loyalty, you aren't indispensable, you know. Get one of the girls from the typing pool to come in and answer the telephone, and get out of here. Enjoy yourself.'

'It's really not necessary—'

He smiled. 'Look, if you don't want to marry me, that's fine, but I don't want your sister thinking that I treat you like a slave, either.' He retreated to his office.

Alisa sat there for an instant in stunned

silence. A man whose proposal of marriage had been rejected just didn't act like that—but he had sounded so matter of fact that it was almost an insult.

'That,' she reminded herself tartly, 'is because it isn't really a marriage he's looking for, it's a corporate merger. And he isn't taking the rejection personally because to him it isn't a personal matter at all!'

She called the typing pool to get someone to cover for her, and she was at the airport early. But, as she paced the concourse and waited for the flight to be called, she couldn't stop thinking about that last comment of his. He had seemed to be more concerned about what Shelley might think of him than he was about Alisa's refusal. His attitude seemed to be that Alisa had been offered a magnificent opportunity; if she didn't want it, then someone else would, and the end result would be much the same as far as he was concerned. He sounded as if all he was doing was hiring another secretary!

Worse than that, she reminded herself.

At least he'd called Alisa's ex-employer for a chat before he'd hired her. What was he planning to do with his final candidates for wifehood—ask them for written references?

'And I don't care,' she muttered, 'as long as he leaves me out of it. He deserves whatever misery he gets!'

She saw Clay first, as the passengers came streaming up the ramp from the big jet. Her first thought was, He's not looking well. Then she realised it was only because she had grown so used to year-round southern tans that Clay's winter pallor looked unhealthy, almost sallow. Beside him, tiny, dark-haired Shelley stopped in the middle of the waiting-room and stood on tiptoe to peer across the crowd, and then rushed to throw her arms around Alisa. She was talking so fast that there was no sense in doing anything but give her a hug.

It was always like that, Alisa thought. Shelley was four years younger, but even in their teenage years it had generally been she who had rattled on about boys and dances and make-up and music. Alisa had listened, and kept her own counsel, and envied her sister sometimes for that dashing approach to life, the assurance that whatever she wanted would be hers if she reached out for it.

And generally that was true, Alisa thought. There was Clay, for instance—she had just put out her hand and snatched him.

That isn't fair, she told herself. In the first place, Clay had had something to say about it; Shelley could hardly have eloped with him if he hadn't been willing. And she probably wouldn't have done it, no matter what, if she had known that Alisa had considered this particular young man her property. Shelley was many things—careless, irresponsible, self-centred—but she wasn't vicious.

No, it couldn't rightly be blamed on Shelley. Alisa had still been holding the special joy of her love for Clay to her heart, not quite ready to share it, when Shelley had come to Green Bay almost exactly a year ago. There had been nothing to share, really, when it came right down to it; they had not been engaged or even promised. But they had started to talk now and then about the future, and about the dreams they'd had in common. It was only a matter of time, Alisa had thought, and she had hugged the precious knowledge close. Soon it would be official, and how delighted Shelley would be when she could share the news!

It wasn't until Clay and Shelley had eloped that Alisa had even begun to suspect the developing attachment between them. Now, she felt like a fool not to have seen it, but then it had all seemed so innocent—Clay keeping Shelley company while Alisa was at work, taking her to see the sights, entertaining her...

They had come back to see her a couple of days after their abrupt wedding, with Shelley excited and bubbling and Clay determined to face the consequences like a man, secure in his love for his wife, confident that Alisa would understand. And what was Alisa to say then, when it was too late? It would do no good for anyone if she told Shelley how foolish she had been, and it would only make her own pain worse. It was bad enough that Clay suspected how much she had been hurt; why increase the agony by describing the details? So she had given them her blessing, and she had made her plans to leave Green Bay.

No, it wasn't Shelley's fault. Shelley had never known about Alisa and Clay. And Shelley would never know, not even if it killed Alisa to keep her secret. She could not destroy her sister's happiness.

So, when Shelley finally released her stranglehold, and Clay said, 'Well, Alisa? How about a hug?' she took her courage in both hands and turned to face him with a welcoming smile, and when he put his arms around her she did not cry out with the pain of remembering the times when his hugs had not been brotherly, when his kisses had not been restrained.

It was the most difficult thing she had ever done in her life.

CHAPTER FIVE

'She's got no common sense, that's the problem,' Justin said flatly. 'A woman called the office yesterday and asked if it was all right, since her husband was the one who moved out and filed for divorce, if she threw all his bowling trophies in the garbage...'

Alisa cradled the telephone against her shoulder and moved the cat aside so she could spoon coffee grounds into the pot. It was still early, but she had a feeling she was going to need the caffeine. The mere fact that Justin had called her at home at this hour was not a good sign.

'And that incredible female from the typing pool told her not to.'

She frowned. 'Isn't that what you'd have said yourself? Surely you wouldn't condone destruction of the man's personal property?'

126

'Yes, it is what I would have told her,' Justin said impatiently. 'But I certainly wouldn't have suggested that instead she send them all to the Salvation Army thrift shop!'

'Oh.' If it hadn't been so serious, Alisa thought, the image would have been a funny one.

'Fortunately, I walked through the office just then, and no permanent damage was done.'

'I'll have a word with the girl. I should never have let her take over.'

He made a noise that might have been agreement.

'You aren't going to fire her, are you, Justin? It's just lack of experience,' she added gently. 'She's only twenty years old.'

'She might acquire experience, if she lives long enough,' he conceded. 'But when she's sixty that woman still won't have any common sense. You are coming in today, aren't you, so I can send her back to the typing pool?' He sounded anxious.

'Of course I'm coming in.' She was

already dressed for work, as a matter of fact, a full hour earlier than usual. The first glimmer of morning light creeping in her bedroom window had found her lying awake and rigid, wretchedly waiting for the moment when she could leave the apartment...

'Good. I am sorry to take you away from your guests, though. What are they going to do today?'

Go home, if I had my choice, Alisa thought. Or perhaps jump off the top of Camelback Mountain...

'I don't know,' she said. 'We haven't had a chance to make plans.'

'Are they going to rent a car? They'll almost have to, if they're going to see anything at all. Unless...' There was a brief, thoughtful silence. 'Tell you what, Mac, I'll pick you up and they can use your car.'

'You aren't really concerned about them, are you, Justin? You just want to be certain I don't change my mind about working.'

He laughed. 'See you in half an hour, Mac.'

Under other circumstances, she thought, that would have been a very thoughtful thing for him to do. As it was... But perhaps, she thought, it wasn't such a bad idea after all; with a car, Clay and Shelley could entertain themselves, and she would have a wonderful excuse—if she was depending on Justin for transportation, then of course she couldn't be expected to leave the office early.

Half an hour, she thought. It would take at least that long for him to drive into the city in rush-hour traffic, but if she was in luck perhaps Clay and Shelley would still be asleep then, and she could just leave a note and the car keys and slip out. She would be very quiet. After all, Shelley had always liked to stay up late and sleep till noon; it would take a lot of noise to wake her. And as for Clay...

As the coffee started to brew, she let the first cup trickle into a heavy china mug and then slid the pot on to the warming tray to collect the rest, remembering the mornings after Clay had stayed over at her apartment when she had made coffee this way because she was too anxious to return to him to wait for the pot to cycle completely. Then she would take a mug back to the bedroom and wave it under his nose, to help wake him up...

She sipped her coffee and turned around to check the kitchen clock, and almost dropped the mug at the sight of Clay standing motionless in the doorway. His hair was rumpled, he was barefoot, and he was wearing pyjama bottoms but no top. The mat of blond hair on his chest lay in tangled curls, and his blue eyes were heavy-lidded. His sensual good looks had always been most evident in the mornings; today he looked great.

It is going to be even more difficult than I expected, Alisa thought wearily. And the knowledge that had burst upon her within an hour of picking them up at the airport wasn't going to help.

Because she knew that Clay wasn't happy.

She couldn't quite say why she was so certain. There was nothing she could put her finger on precisely, but there was a shadow in his eyes, a strain in his smile, a little break sometimes in his voice, as if he was preoccupied.

It's because he's here, she had told herself. He doesn't like this any more than I do—this unspoken agreement between us to make sure Shelley doesn't suspect. Two weeks—the stress is on him, too.

But that wasn't it at all, she had concluded by the time they had picked up the luggage and ordered lunch at a delightful little restaurant near the airport. It wasn't when he was talking to Alisa that the tension showed. Then he was charming and calm, and there was no strained note in his laughter, as there was when he looked at his wife.

Alisa tried to tell herself that it was only wishful thinking that made her see the trouble in his eyes—her own desires telling her that he couldn't possibly be as happy with Shelley as he could have been with her. After all, this image didn't fit at all; Shelley had told her how happy Clay was about the baby coming.

Perhaps, she thought bleakly, Shelley

doesn't know how unhappy he is. Perhaps she can't even see that there's a problem...

Clay ran a hand through his hair. 'You still can't wait for your coffee in the morning, can you?' His voice was a gravelly, sexy murmur at this hour.

He's scarcely awake, she thought. It's hardly fair to blame the man for the tactless reminder of other days, when he hardly has his eyes open yet.

But the allusion stung, anyway. She got another mug down from the cabinet and filled it for him, wordlessly, then led the way to the tiny table in the dining-room.

'Was that your new man on the phone?' There was a teasing note in his voice. 'Shelley is convinced there must be one.'

How long had he been standing there, anyway? Alisa wondered. How much of the conversation had he overheard? 'Don't you start on me, too,' she said, trying to keep her voice light. 'That was my boss.'

He nodded. He cradled the mug in his big hand and took a long swallow. 'Seems to me anyone who calls at this hour of the morning is pretty certain of his reception.'

'Or just self-confident in general,' Alisa countered coolly. 'Which is the case with Justin. Why is Shelley so certain there's a new man in my life, anyway?'

'Because you so obviously don't want to talk about it.'

'Well, I wish she'd give the subject a decent burial—she certainly beat it to death all day yesterday. Just because I haven't been home a few times when she thought I should be, she's concluded I'm hiding a new love interest.'

'Are you, Alisa?'

It was a soft, husky question, enough to make her insides go all quivery, and the teasing note was gone. Did he truly care? she asked herself helplessly. Was it possible...?

She clenched her fist, under the edge of the table, until her manicured nails cut crescents in her palm, and then she said calmly, 'I really don't think that's your business, Clay.'

Clay grinned. But was there a shadow

behind the gleam in his eyes? 'You always were the prim and proper one, weren't you, Alisa?'

If I was, she thought, then why did you marry Shelley when you only slept with me?

A rustle from the living-room warned her, and she was wearing a smile when she turned to greet Shelley. She was fresh from sleep, and she looked innocent and years younger than her actual age. Her hair was still uncombed, and she was wearing a huge nightshirt emblazoned over the abdomen with an anatomically correct sketch of an unborn infant.

At least it's only a nightshirt, Alisa told herself faintly. She could have decided to start wearing maternity clothes already.

Shelley's face fell at the sight of Alisa's soft blue suit and ruffled blouse. 'You're actually going to work today?'

'I do have to make a living.'

'But we've only just got here. Can't you call in sick, darling?'

Alisa wasn't going to get into that argument. 'Why don't you decide today what you'd like to do over the weekend?' she suggested instead. 'I'll call you this afternoon, and if we need reservations or anything I can take care of it from the office.'

'But what are we supposed to do today?' Shelley wailed.

'You could start by cooking my breakfast,' Clay suggested.

Shelley gave him a smothering glance. 'If you're starving, fix something for yourself. I don't plan to spend my vacation in the kitchen, and I don't want to sit around an apartment all the time. I had no idea you lived so far from everything, Alisa.'

That answers my question, Alisa thought. She does know that something is wrong, that Clay isn't happy. This isn't the Shelley I used to know—this catty, sharp-voiced woman... But the knowledge didn't quite take away her half-formed desire to slap Shelley across her pretty face and tell her to stop behaving like a spoilt brat.

'You can have my car today,' Alisa said, and thought, Bless Justin.

'Well, that certainly helps.' It was matter

of fact. 'Where would you suggest I start shopping? I want to buy some things for the baby.'

Clay took his head out of the refrigerator. 'It's a little early for that, Shelley.'

'Just some things for the nursery,' Shelley said, with a charming little pout. She followed him and rubbed her cheek against his arm. 'Some little, tiny things.'

'I'm much more flexible when I'm not hungry,' Clay pointed out.

Shelley eyed him silently for a moment and then started taking things out of the refrigerator. 'Sausage and eggs, I suppose? You don't even care that the smell of breakfast cooking makes me feel nauseous these days, do you? Well, aren't you lucky—I see Alisa buys the brand of sausage you like best.'

Alisa closed her eyes for an instant in pain. I had forgotten, she thought. I wonder how many other things I still buy because Clay liked them best. 'How fortunate that it was on sale this week,' she said lightly, and escaped to answer the door.

136

Justin still had his finger on the bell. 'I didn't think your neighbours would like it if I sat in the car park and made noises like a siren till you came down.'

'Sorry—I meant to be downstairs waiting for you.'

'That's all right. I wanted to meet your sister anyway, so she'd remember my angelic face and take you with a pinch of salt when you start telling her what a demanding boss I am.'

Both Clay and Shelley had come into the living-room by then. Shelley was obviously assessing the cut of Justin's dark-grey suit and the fact that his white shirt was silk; Clay leaned quietly against the back of a chair and watched.

Justin shook hands with both of them and politely ignored their half-dressed state. 'I hope you'll like Phoenix,' he said. 'If there is anything I can do to help you enjoy yourselves...'

Alisa wanted to groan.

Shelley batted her big eyes and said, 'How lovely of you! I'm sure you know all the really wonderful places to eat.'

Justin laughed. 'I think I've tried every one of them, yes. May I take you all out to dinner tonight?'

Shelley accepted with glee.

Alisa waited till she was safely in the Cadillac before saying, with considerable restraint, 'Perhaps I should warn you that Shelley is not the kind who would see the charm of Emilio's Bar and Grill.'

'I suspected that,' Justin said gravely. 'You're sisters, hmm?'

'Half-sisters, technically.' She was looking out of the window; Phoenix was speeding by at what seemed a phenomenal rate. Justin was obviously anxious to get to the office.

'Oh, that explains it.' He sounded preoccupied. 'There's not much resemblance between you.'

Alisa twisted around to stare at him. You shouldn't be surprised, she told herself. It's a rare man who doesn't admire Shelley's type—the dark hair, the big eyes, the pretty face. We blondes have a hard time of it, she thought; when we don't wear make-up it looks as if we don't even have eyelashes, much less the long, curly, sexy kind that Shelley was born with.

But she had long ago got used to that fact. It certainly wasn't Shelley's fault that she was so blindingly lovely, that she was all the things Alisa would never be.

'Do you have the same mother? Or father?' Justin asked.

'Mother. She married Matthew Rhodes just a few months after she divorced my father, and Shelley was born about a year later.' She waited for him to say something cutting about people who fell out of love.

Instead, his voice was gentle. 'It's tough to lose a parent and have a stepfather, isn't it?'

'Matt has always been very good to me,' Alisa said stiffly. 'And I was only three when he married my mother. I don't remember it being any other way.'

They reached the office just then, and she was grateful that there was no chance for him to press the subject. He paused beside her desk. 'You might give Great-Aunt Louise a call today,' he suggested.

'Telephone her? Why on earth?' She

was already flipping through the mail; she looked up in surprise. 'And why me? Oh, I know—you've found a martyr to agree to be your wife, and you want me to break the news.'

He frowned. 'Mac, don't you think that's a little harsh? I don't see why you'd consider "martyr" the right term at all. And no, I haven't.'

'Then why—?'

'You'll find a telegram from her in that mess somewhere,' he said gently. 'It seems that you didn't write my letter to her on Monday—'

'I forgot it completely. Besides, I had no idea what to say to her, under the circumstances—'

'And I forgot that I hadn't signed one, and so I didn't ask you about it, and—'

'How touching! She's worried about you.'

'No, as a matter of fact she's worried about *you*. Obviously your efforts to write letters from my point of view haven't been as successful as we'd hoped.'

Alisa scrabbled through the pile of mail

till she found the pale yellow Western Union envelope. 'Dear Justin, Hope your secretary's illness not severe,' she read aloud. 'Looking forward to her next letter. Louise.' She put the telegram down. 'Well, I'm glad she enjoys my efforts. And not a personal word for you, Justin—not that you deserve it, when you don't even bother to read those letters before you sign them.'

'I do too read them!' he complained.

'Well, I wouldn't blame her if she does ignore your birthday next year, if you can't even send her a personal thanks for a generous gift. Oh, that reminds me.' She reached for her handbag and gave him a tiny, gaily wrapped package.

Justin frowned at it.

'Don't get crazy. It's not a birthday gift, exactly.'

'Then what is it?' He pulled the paper off as cautiously as if he expected the package to bite him. 'A cassette tape of funny messages for an answering machine? Thanks, but—'

'I thought that would be the next logical piece of equipment for your car—a machine to take messages when you aren't there to answer your new telephone.' She smiled brightly. 'I'd have bought you the machine, but my budget is a bit tight this month.'

He turned the tape over. 'I don't take hints when it comes to rises, Mac.'

'So much for the possibility of your feeling generous after the disaster yesterday!'

'Put it in writing and I'll consider it.'

'And then turn me down, I suppose. You deserve the girl from the typing pool.'

He grinned at her and started across to his office. 'Don't threaten me. I already know that a really good secretary is hard to find.'

'I've got it!' she said on a note of discovery. 'You could marry *her.*'

He wheeled around at the door of his office, so suddenly that he almost lost his balance. The look of horror in his eyes spoke volumes.

'Didn't you say you were looking for a woman who'd give up her job to stay home and raise kids?' Alisa asked. 'She'd be perfect. Everybody seems to agree that she shouldn't spend all her life in an office—'

He slammed his door. Alisa smiled and composed a memo asking for a rise, and the letter giving it to her, just in case he decided to be agreeable. After all, there was no harm in asking, and she suspected that for the next two weeks her bills were likely to resemble the national defence budget. She was going to need all the help she could get.

The French restaurant Justin had chosen was tucked away in a corner of the Kendrick Hotel, Phoenix's newest and most luxurious resort. The restaurant was small and intimate and obviously expensive. Shelley took one look around the elegant lounge and murmured, 'Now this is the kind of guy you should hang on to, Alisa.' She fluttered over to the corner table where he was waiting for them.

Alisa could almost feel Clay's dejected sigh. She sneaked a look up at him under her lashes, and felt sorry for him when he said, 'My wife seems to think I'm a hick.'

'She didn't mean it that way, Clay. Sometimes Shelley just doesn't think before she speaks.'

He looked down at her for a long moment, and then said, so softly that she wasn't absolutely certain she had caught each word, 'I know. But some days, Alisa, I wonder if I've made a very bad mistake—and if I'll be paying for it all my life.'

Then Justin was rising from the table to greet them, and there was a flurry of chair-holding and drink-ordering and small talk. Alisa contributed her share automatically. She was still thinking about that whispered half-confession.

What did it mean? What could it mean? Was he just irritated at Shelley tonight, or was he truly disillusioned? Shelley was different, that was certain—she had changed dramatically from the warm-hearted girl he had married. Living with her—well, after just two days in her company Alisa was ready for a break.

She couldn't blame Clay for being tired of it, after a year...

'When they fall out of love,' Justin had said, 'a lot of partners find they can't stand each other and call it quits.' Was that what would happen to Shelley and Clay? And if it did, what would that mean to Alisa? The man she loved would be free, then...

And she herself would always be seen as the woman who had stolen her sister's husband, who had deliberately destroyed a marriage in order to have the man she wanted. Shelley would certainly see it that way, and the pain, the hint of guilt for having hurt her so badly, would haunt them always.

And then, there was the baby—Shelley's baby, and Clay's. For an instant, Alisa had forgotten all about the innocent child who would be caught up in the mess. She had seen too many bitter custody battles, too many arguments over a parent's rights and responsibilities, to help to create such a situation herself.

No, whatever happened to her sister's marriage, it could make no difference to Alisa. If Clay's choice had been a mistake, it was an irretrievable one now. They would get through the rest of this visit the best way they could, and she would make sure, no matter what it took, that this painful episode would never be repeated. It would be better for everyone that way.

She glanced at him over the rim of her champagne glass, and thought, Goodbye, my love. There is no hope for us...

'I love this weather,' Shelley was saying. 'I adore running around in March dressed in practically nothing. It's so warm down here.'

Justin's gaze met Alisa's as he gravely agreed, and when she saw the smile in his eyes she had to fight to keep her own face straight. It had been cloudy all day; to a native, it was unseasonably cool. Only to a snowbird like Shelley, fresh from a northern winter, would today seem like summer.

How quickly I've grown accustomed to the climate, Alisa thought. And how rude it is of me to laugh at my sister. She's such a child herself sometimes—with a child's impatience and a child's enthusiasm—how could I even have considered allowing that to be destroyed?

The realisation of how selfish she was capable of being left Alisa a bit chastened, and a little quieter than usual. She contented herself with smiling a lot, and listening to the others' conversation.

When they went into the dining-room Shelley took one look at the menu and exclaimed in delight. 'Green Bay has nothing that can compare to this,' she confided. 'You know, if it only weren't so spread out, Phoenix would be perfect.'

Justin laughed. 'But it has to be big to have room for all the wonderful things it contains,' he reminded, and Shelley laughed and playfully patted his hand.

Alisa gave Justin credit; he'd certainly chosen the perfect place to impress the girl. And he knew exactly how to entertain her, too, without quite stepping over the line into flirtation. When she asked him if he'd ever handled the divorces of any celebrities, he told her a wickedly funny story about a gossip columnist and a Hollywood star who had battled it out in the courts—and the newspapers—for years, and only smiled and shook his head when she tried to guess who they were.

Clay, meanwhile, was growing more morosely silent by the minute, and was drinking a great deal more wine than was good for him. When, over the veal escalopes, Justin asked him about his line of work, he said shortly, 'I'm in middle management at a factory, spending my days shuffling paper with no prospect for advancement. Please, don't remind me of it—I'm on vacation.'

Alisa was startled at the bitterness in his voice.

'Clay, don't be such a wet blanket,' Shelley scolded. 'It's all going to work out you know it will.' She turned back to Justin. 'Clay's wonderful at dealing with people, but his present job doesn't let him have that chance. He'd really like to have a little business of his own where he can work directly with people—'

'Instead of with invoices and statistics

and production runs,' Clay finished. 'Let's talk about something else, all right?'

It wasn't much later when Shelley excused herself to go the ladies' room. When she hadn't returned a couple of minutes later, Alisa followed.

She found her sister sitting in the corner of the plush little lounge. She was apparently staring at an odd pattern in the watered-silk wall-covering, and she didn't seem to hear anything until Alisa was standing beside her. Then she looked up with a forced smile and said, 'I like your Justin, darling. I'd recommend you go after him with both hands, before some other woman comes along and snaps him up. Of course you've got the advantage, but—'

'Shelley...' It was almost hesitant. If she and Clay are having marital problems, Alisa thought, I'm not sure I want to know. But it's so apparent that there is something badly wrong... 'Do you want to talk about it?'

'About what, dear?' Shelley pulled herself up out of her chair and started to powder her nose.

'Whatever is bothering you, that's what. If you're in trouble—'

'Oh, it's just this frightful nausea. I don't know why they call it morning sickness, you know, as if it actually goes away as soon as the clock strikes noon. What a joke! I'm miserable all the time.' She leaned towards the mirror to inspect the poreless perfection of her skin.

'But think about the baby,' Alisa said gently. 'Try not to dwell on how wretched you're feeling—'

'That's easy for you to say. You haven't felt it.'

And I probably never will, Alisa thought. She bit her lip and said calmly, 'Concentrate on how wonderful it will be when the baby comes. It will be worth all the misery, then, the first time you hold your own child.'

'Sometimes,' Shelley said distantly, 'I wonder.' Then she looked up and laughed. 'I'm expecting to have the first two-year-long pregnancy in the history of the world, you know—it seems that it's already been going on for months and months!' She led the way back to the table, and she did not lose control of the conversation again, despite the pallor that no amount of animation could quite conceal.

When the valet brought the cars round after dinner, Shelley eyed the Cadillac convertible. 'What a luscious car,' she told Justin. 'May I have a ride in it some time?'

'How about right now? I'll take you home.'

'Don't be ridiculous,' Alisa said sharply. 'It's miles out of your way, Justin—'

'After thirty years of living in Phoenix, Mac—' Justin grimaced and added '—all right, thirty-five years—I've concluded that everything is out of the way.' He tucked Shelley into the passenger seat.

'See?' she said. 'I told you the place was spread out!'

The Cadillac slipped neatly into traffic.

'Guess we're on our own,' Clay said. He took the keys to Alisa's little car from the valet. He drove slowly, not yet used to the city's traffic patterns. She was too conscious of the silence to do much more than give directions now and then, when he was uncertain of himself.

'I don't think your friend Justin likes me much,' Clay said finally. 'And I have to say I'm not fond of him either.'

Alisa sent a stricken look at him. The street lights sent bars of shadow across his face, and over his hands, which were clenched on the steering-wheel. 'Clay, it was nothing, really. He was just being a good host, and I'm sure Shelley doesn't take it seriously, either.'

He made a noise that sounded like a discouraged grunt.

She felt herself vindicated a couple of minutes later, after they reached the apartment and Justin refused coffee and went home, when Shelley asked Clay to go for a walk with her.

For a moment, he didn't answer.

'Why not?' Alisa said. 'There's a beautiful moon, and the fresh air would do you both good.'

Clay's mouth twisted a little, but the two of them went off together, and Alisa tried to smother a sigh of relief.

She took a long shower and was already in bed when they came back, but she could hear the murmur of conversation and the tiny domestic noises as they settled down for the night. She tried to be grateful—for the baby's sake, if for no other reason—that everything had been patched back together once more. But it was hard.

The baby, she thought. She had thought for a moment tonight that if Shelley had a choice right now she'd hand over her baby without a second of hesitation. The idea made Alisa feel almost as sick as Shelley seemed to be.

I'd put up with all the misery in the world, she thought, to be in her shoes. But it will never happen to me. I will never hold my own baby in my arms, and say, Yes, it was worth it all to have this tiny, precious child.

Unless... There was Justin.

She turned on to her stomach and pulled the pillow over her head. That, she told herself furiously, is quite possibly the most insane idea you have ever allowed to cross your mind! You wouldn't want to share that experience with anyone but Clay. Marriage, home, children—those things are meaningless unless they're shared with the man you love.

But if it was impossible to have the man she loved, then what? Was she forever condemned to be alone?

What was it Justin had said? 'People insist on thinking that if they can't have that one perfect person, nothing else is worth considering...'

The image of a baby, dark-haired, sweet, tiny, trusting, was so real that for an instant she could almost feel the softness of a blanketed bundle nestling close to her breast. A child of her own—was that so much to ask of life?

Thousands of people raised children alone, without their partners. Some of them had deliberately made the choice to be a single parent. Not me, Alisa thought. That's not the way I want it to be. And yet...

You can't marry without love, she told herself ruthlessly. To do so would be to cheat the man you marry.

Unless that man was Justin Abernathy. He would not feel cheated, because that would be exactly the arrangement he wanted. If she married Justin...

Out of the question, she told herself. In any case, he's already reconsidered it, after his experience with the girl from the typing pool yesterday. Candidates for wifehood were one thing, but a really good secretary was hard to find...

She yawned, and told herself that strange things happened in the mind while it disconnected itself on the way to sleep. That was all this was—the electrical misfirings of an exhausted brain.

Her last conscious thought was of Shelley. It didn't concern the baby, and it didn't involve Clay. She was wondering instead, as she slid into sleep, just what it was that Justin thought of Shelley. He'd certainly been paying enough attention to her...

CHAPTER SIX

It was a relief to go back to work on Monday, even though the weekend had been reasonably pleasant, all things considered. There had been no outbursts of temper and no calamities; Shelley appeared to be much calmer, and even her morning sickness seemed to have let up.

Or else, Alisa thought, she's just made up her mind not to let it interfere with the really important things—like shopping.

That's catty, she told herself. You shouldn't think such things about your sister.

Nevertheless, it was nice to get back into the ordinary routine. And to think, she told herself, just a couple of weeks ago going to work was the only exciting part of my life. Now it's more like retreating into a sanctuary...

On Monday morning, Justin stopped to

pick her up again. This time he arrived in time to drink a cup of coffee, play with the Siamese cat, and chat with Clay, who swallowed his dislike enough to thank Justin for his thoughtfulness. 'It was nice for us to have Alisa's car on Friday,' he said.

'Being stuck anywhere in Phoenix without a car is a fate no one should be sentenced to suffer,' Justin told him gravely. He turned the cat upside down in his arms and scratched the animal's chin; Vibrato stretched his neck out and then yawned, looking enormously pleased with himself.

Alisa finished rinsing and stacking the dishes that were left in the sink from bedtime snacks and breakfast. 'I'll leave the coffee for Shelley when she wakes up,' she told Clay. 'But please remember to turn the pot off when you leave.' She dried her hands, slipped into the tweed jacket of her suit, and picked up her handbag. 'Sorry to keep you waiting, Justin.'

He put the cat down, much to Vibrato's displeasure, and brushed a few stray cream-coloured hairs off the sleeve of his navy pin-striped jacket. He didn't comment.

The next day, Shelley was up when Justin arrived; she entertained him in the living-room while Alisa finished drying a load of bath towels.

When he came on Wednesday, Alisa was changing the sheets in the extra bedroom; her guests were already gone. Clay, despite his distaste for early rising, had been eager to see how the desert looked at dawn; Shelley had grumbled but had gone along, after extracting a promise of lunch at the French restaurant where Justin had taken them.

By Thursday, it seemed to Alisa that the ordeal had been going on somewhat longer than the Hundred Years War. And when Justin chose that morning to turn down her request for a rise in salary it felt like the last straw.

'Suddenly acquiring two hangers-on is not an adequate reason to ask for more money,' he said, when he called her into his office to tell her his decision.

If she'd had a letter opener, she'd have thrown it at him—which, she supposed, was why he hadn't told her while she was sitting at her own desk. 'They aren't hangers-on,' she said stiffly.

He looked at a seam in the panelling just above her head and asked thoughtfully, 'In the week he's been driving your car, has Clay put any fuel in it?'

'No.'

'And from what I've seen with my own eyes, I'd guess neither of them has lifted a hand around the apartment, either.'

'I thought you liked Shelley, at least.'

'I'm not blind, Mac.' He straightened a stack of documents on the corner of his desk and added, a little more gently, 'How do you plan to get through another whole week of watching their marriage fall apart?'

'It's not falling apart.'

He lifted one eyebrow and said, 'I wouldn't say they've become the best of friends, would you?'

'You and your damned theories!' she began, and then decided that there were

159

better ways to deal with Justin. 'By the way,' she added sweetly, 'how is your campaign to find a wife going? Have you selected the finalists yet?'

He glared at her and tossed a business card across the desk. 'Thanks for reminding me. Would you send flowers to this address today, please?'

Alisa looked at it with raised eyebrows. 'You're sending flowers to Ridge Coltrain? The Goulds must have settled all their quarrels in record time—'

'On the back, Alisa.'

She turned the card over. There was not only an address, scrawled in the bold black ink that Ridge preferred, but a name and a telephone number. She glanced up at Justin from under raised eyebrows. 'Long-stemmed red roses, I presume?'

'Not roses. Plain pink carnations would be just fine.'

'Mere carnations for a girl named Desirée? If you want her to be available next time you call—'

'Since I'm not planning to call her again, it's a matter of indifference to me whether she stays home and waits for the telephone to ring. If she wasn't Ridge's cousin, I wouldn't bother to send the flowers.'

I think I'd like to meet Desirée, she thought. She sounds like just the sort of thing he deserves. 'Ridge is a very good lawyer,' she said, with an air of fairness. 'You shouldn't expect him to be a matchmaker of equal aptitude. I don't suppose you would like it any better if I sent forget-me-nots?'

He was growling as she gently closed the door behind her. She hadn't seen him lose his temper in a good long time, and she found it a bit amusing that it was his theory of marriage that was causing the trouble. He was obviously finding this whole thing more difficult than he had expected.

Before the day was out, however, she had begun to regret giving in to the impulse to bait him. It had been a more than usually frustrating day. At mid-morning a couple who had come in like love-birds to sign their pre-nuptial agreement literally came to blows in Justin's office when the groom-to-be made a jocular comment that the prospective bride took as an insult. Just after lunch a woman who had written up her own divorce papers in order to save some money got hysterical when Justin told her she had signed away all her rights to her husband's profit-sharing fund, and it was too late to do anything about it. The icing on the cake was at mid-afternoon, when Justin was ushering a grief-stricken woman out of his office—a woman whose small daughter had been kidnapped by her father after a weekend visitation—and saw that Debbie Baxter was waiting for him. Today she was wearing a brief pink tennis dress, and her racket was on the table beside her.

He turned a glare on Alisa that should have wilted her in her chair. She frowned back and said, 'I told Mrs Baxter that your appointment schedule is full, but she said she'd be happy to wait.' And don't blame me for it, she wanted to add. I can't push a button and eject her through the roof!

Debbie put down her magazine and said, 'Justin, darling! I've tried and tried to catch you, but you're such a busy boy—you're just never at home any more, are you? I simply have to talk to you.'

'Mac, make an appointment for—'

'But it's an emergency, Justin. Bob is being a stickler about my alimony all of a sudden, and I'm afraid that we'll have to go to court again.' She dabbed at the corner of her eye with a tissue. 'If you could just set my mind at rest—I can't concentrate on anything!'

Even tennis, Alisa wanted to murmur with pseudo-sympathy.

'All right. Come on in, Debbie.' Behind her back, he caught Alisa's eye and held up a hand, fingers spread wide. She nodded.

Precisely five minutes later, she pushed the intercom button and said, 'I'm sorry to bother you, Mr Abernathy, but you asked me to let you know when Mr Johnson arrived.'

His crisply mechanical voice thanked her, and less than a minute later Debbie appeared again, with Justin right behind her. 'Sorry,' he was saying. 'We'll have to finish this another time.'

The redhead looked at the empty chairs and said, sounding slightly sulky, 'Mr Johnson, hmm?'

'He's waiting in the conference-room,' Alisa said smoothly. 'Here's the file.' She handed Justin an official-looking folder that happened to be full of blank letterhead, and turned back to the property settlement that was spread on her desk for its last proof-reading.

As the door closed behind them, she heard Debbie say, 'I've got an extra ticket to that wonderful concert tonight, too—you know, the pianist who's supposed to be the new Sol Abrams. I thought if you weren't busy, darling...'

A couple of minutes later Justin was back. He tossed the folder on to Alisa's desk and said, 'Next time we need a fictitious client, don't say he's in the conference-room—you can see the door from the reception area, and if it happened to be standing open we'd be dead.'

'That's why I went and closed it before I called you,' she murmured.

A slow smile lit his face. 'You are a jewel,

Mac. Do I have any more appointments?'

Alisa shook her head.

'Then I'm going to the gym for a while to work off some frustration.'

He was gone before she could remind him that she was depending on him for a ride home. She turned back to her paperwork, wistfully hoping that he wouldn't forget. She could always call a taxi, but with the state of her bank account she'd rather not.

Her hope for a peaceful finish to the day was splintered half an hour before the office closed when Shelley called, so excited that her words were running together in an incoherent mass.

'Hold on!' Alisa commanded. 'Slow down! If I didn't know better I'd think you just told me that you and Clay bought a store this afternoon—'

'We did.'Shelley giggled. 'Well, part-interest in it. It's a women's clothing boutique—just the kind of thing Clay's always wanted. The owner is retiring, and we can buy it from him on time payments so some day we'll own it all. Isn't it wonderful, darling? We were beginning to detest the idea of going home to the cold weather and Clay's hateful job. And then this came along, just like magic, Alisa—as if it was meant to be!'

Alisa shifted her grip on the telephone and said desperately, 'You can't be serious, Shelley. You can't make important decisions like this so quickly—'

'We didn't, really,' Shelley said ingenuously. 'We stumbled across the opportunity on Monday, so we've been thinking about it for days. And of course we called Daddy and asked his opinion before we signed the papers. It will be so much better for Clay to be away from that dreadful job in Green Bay. And I'm looking forward to being a real Arizona girl.'

They can't stay in Phoenix, Alisa thought. They just can't. I won't allow it—

Allow it? she asked herself hollowly. How on earth are you planning to prevent it?

'One of the reasons I called,' Shelley went on in a confidential tone, 'is to say that if there's something you'd like to do tonight—well, don't turn it down for our sake. We've got a lot to celebrate, and if you don't mind—'

'You'd like to be alone,' Alisa finished. There was a harsh edge to her voice.

'I know it's awful of me.' Shelley's voice was wheedling and sympathetic all at once. 'It's your apartment, after all. But it would be so nice to have just a bit of privacy...'

'Will it be safe if I come home at nine?' Alisa asked, and was even more irritated when Shelley didn't seem to hear the sarcasm.

She put the telephone down and dropped her face into her shaking hands. You won't have to see much of them, she told herself, grasping desperately for the positive side of things. They'll be busy with this new business. And chances are when they get an apartment of their own it won't even be near yours.

But when, she asked herself wretchedly, would that be? She could scarcely evict them when they were, in a sense, her invited guests, and it might be a month or more before they found a place and actually moved. From the sounds of things, any cash they might have had was now tied up in the boutique...

They can't stay in Phoenix, she thought. It isn't fair. It isn't right.

But there was no way around it. There was nothing she could do to prevent it. So she groaned. It didn't change things, but it relieved her tension a bit.

'Miss McClenaghan?' The receptionist sounded startled. 'Are you feeling all right? I just came in to ask if you needed a ride, since Mr Abernathy hasn't come back.'

Alisa thought about saying, Yes—you can drop me off at Pitcairn Island. That should be far enough away.

Mechanically, she began to put papers away, shoving them at random into folders, pushing the folders into the drawers of her desk. 'That's very thoughtful of you,' she said. 'I do have a headache.'

The receptionist clucked sympathetically. 'You should go straight home and lie down in a darkened room.'

'I've been told it's best to keep busy.'

But doing what? she wondered. From now until nine o'clock... Me and my big mouth! Why didn't I just tell Shelley that if she wanted privacy she could rent a hotel room?

'Who gave you that crazy advice? Mr Abernathy? It sounds like him.'

Advice, Alisa thought. Mr Abernathy...

A few minutes later the receptionist stopped her car in front of an old building just a few blocks from the law office and looked doubtfully at Alisa. 'I think you're nuts, you know,' she said. 'Why do you want to be dropped off at a place like this?' She waved a hand at the battered façade of the building. A peeling sign announced that Carlson's Gym occupied the top floor.

Alisa looked at it a little doubtfully herself, and then said firmly, 'Because there are some things Mr Abernathy forgot at the office.'

'You couldn't leave them on his desk?' the receptionist called after her.

Alisa ran up the stairs before she had a chance to lose her nerve. At the top she was confronted by a short, balding man chewing a cigar. 'Justin Abernathy,' he repeated thoughtfully, as if he'd never heard the name before. 'He might be here, or he might not. Who's looking for him?'

'I'm his secretary. And don't give me any more nonsense about whether he's here, because his car is parked out front.' It was pleasant, but firm; she had dealt with this sort of man before.

His eyes warmed. 'So you're his Miss Mac,' he said. 'He's in there.' He jerked a thumb over his shoulder.

The room he indicated was huge, and in the centre of it was a boxing ring where two men were sparring. Alisa stopped dead on the threshold.

She scarcely recognised Justin under all the protective gear, but she had to admit that what she could see was impressive—a broad, tanned chest with a mat of reddish-brown hair, well-muscled arms and legs.

Of course, she thought. Justin would never belong to an ordinary health club. Five minutes ago she would have guessed that his choice would be entirely stainless steel with the most modern equipment known to physical fitness experts. But she had forgotten about Emilio's, or she would not have been surprised to find him at a dump with a boxing ring instead. Somehow, it fitted.

The other man in the ring was the first to spot her. He spat out his mouthpiece and called, 'Hey, Carlson! What's the dame doing in here?'

'Mac?' Justin said indistinctly. He leaned on the rope at the edge of the ring. 'Don't tell me you actually forgot something!'

She shifted uneasily from one foot to the other and toyed with the fastener of her leather shoulder-bag. Suddenly she realised how ludicrous it was for her to be here, in this bastion of masculinity. How perfectly foolish it had been to pursue him like this—as if it couldn't wait.

'It was only—' She stopped, and turned away, her head down. 'It was nothing, Justin.'

He slipped between the ropes and followed her. 'Mac...' His voice was suddenly gentle. 'It must have been something.'

She looked up at him. She could almost feel waves of heat from his body, warm from the exercise. His hair was darkened with perspiration, and it curled a little. He reached out, as if he had forgotten the boxing-gloves he wore, and then dropped his hands.

'If it can wait five minutes till I've had a shower,' he said, 'I'll take you someplace quiet and buy you a drink.'

She nodded, grateful for his perception, and then said, 'No, I don't want to interrupt—'

He grinned. 'I was ready to quit anyway, before my youthful beauty got smashed,' he confided. 'He's a great deal better than I am.'

His hair was still damp and curly a few minutes later when they crossed the street to a little restaurant, and he hadn't bothered to put his tie and jacket on.

He ordered the cup of coffee she asked for, and then took a long drink from his beer and set the glass down. 'Fluid replacement,' he said, with a smile.

'I'm stunned, you know. Boxing? I thought you went to the gym to lift weights or something.'

'It's a legitimate sport, Mac. Hardly the same as street brawling.'

'I suppose so,' she said uncertainly. 'But why? It doesn't seem quite your sort of thing.'

He shrugged. 'My father taught me the basics when I was little. He always said if a man knew how to fight, he wouldn't be afraid to—and if he wasn't afraid, he'd find that he didn't need to fight very often. It's the cowards who get hurt, he told me.'

She thought about it. 'Because they're always trying to prove themselves?'

'Something like that. I've found that his philosophy is pretty much true of the law, too. If you're not afraid of a fight, most of the time the problem can be settled without going into court. But if you're not ready—'

'Your father,' she said softly. 'You've never said anything about your family, really. Just Great-Aunt Louise.'

'Isn't Great-Aunt Louise enough, all by herself? What's bothering you, Mac?'

She cupped the heavy pottery mug between her hands and told him about Shelley's call. When she had finished, there was a long silence. She glanced at him once; he was drawing circles on the table with the moisture that had gathered on his glass.

He looked up then. 'It's driving you nuts, isn't it? Having them underfoot all the time, taking advantage of you? You could put an end to it if you really wanted to, you know.'

She stared down into her cup; the coffee was the same colour as his eyes, but it was softer and warmer. Thank heaven he doesn't know it all, she thought. 'I can't just pack their bags and throw them out,' she said. 'No matter how anxious they are to have a place of their own, it will take a little while to arrange it.'

'And what if they aren't anxious to give up all the advantages of living at your place? How long are you going to put up with this?'

'I'm not going to encourage them to stay, that's for sure.' She tried to keep her voice light. 'You wouldn't want to rent out a couple of rooms in your house for a month or two? You've certainly got enough space; you'd probably never notice they were there—'

He shook his head. 'Don't try to pass your problem guests off on me.'

'You won't do it? Not even to keep your secretary happy?'

'I haven't got around to furnishing the spare bedrooms yet, and I doubt a comfort-loving kitten like Shelley would appreciate a sleeping-bag on the floor.'

'It was worth a try,' Alisa murmured. The waitress refilled her cup, and she inhaled the wonderful fragrance of dark-roasted, well-brewed coffee. Justin knew the most amazing places, she reflected. Who would have thought that this little hole-in-the-wall would serve the best cup of coffee she'd ever tasted?

'Besides, if I'm choosing room-mates, I'd much rather have you.'

It was bland, and for a moment Alisa

thought she hadn't heard properly. 'I thought you'd reconsidered,' she said.

'Because I haven't been asking you every fifteen minutes if you've changed your mind? That was just showing respect, Mac. You turned me down, and I accepted that. But if you'd like to think it over—'

'You said you couldn't do without me in the office.'

'I said it would be a problem,' he corrected. 'But when I really thought about it—well, you probably wouldn't quit right away, would you? You might like to work part time for a while, and that would mean you could hire someone and train her—'

'Justin, you're incorrigible.'

'Come on, Mac. What's so ridiculous about it? It still makes sense, you know.'

'Oh? My intuition tells me that women aren't exactly standing in line to apply for the position.'

He looked at her reproachfully. 'Mac, I never expected you to be unkind.'

'Perhaps your standards are just too exacting,' she said helpfully. 'What *was* wrong with Desirée, anyway?'

'Over cocktails, she told me the history of her last failed love-affair. Over the soup, she shed a couple of tears as she gave me the details about the one before that, and—'

'I see. Well, perhaps she has a minor fault or two—'

'A minor fault or two? Mac, I'm looking for someone with enough sense to live today instead of mooning over yesterday or dreaming of next week. As a result, I'm afraid it's going to take longer than I expected, and in the meantime there are problems like Debbie.'

'Oh, yes. Don't forget your date for the concert tonight.'

He grimaced. 'I am not going to the concert—or anything else. But Debbie doesn't seem to get the message.'

'"You could put an end to it if you really wanted to,"' she quoted with a slightly malicious smile. 'Or—I've got it. I'll break the news to Debbie, if you'll invite Shelley and Clay to leave my apartment—'

'There's an easier solution to both problems,' he interrupted.

'Marry you,' Alisa finished. 'You're getting desperate, aren't you?'

'Of course not. It's just the most sensible idea yet. You've been around, right? Surely you've dated more men than just the klutz in Green Bay?'

She asked curiously, 'Why do you call him that?'

'Because he had to be clumsy to let a jewel like you escape him. I'm serious, Mac. How many men have you dated?'

'Several,' she said coolly. 'Why?'

'Don't freeze up. I'm not asking for details *à la* Desiree, believe me. Could you talk to them—really tell them what you were thinking? Could you truly be honest with any of them?'

She thought about it.

He answered his own question. 'Of course not. It's another disaster that the romance myth causes—we should never hurt the feelings of the person we love, so we tiptoe around subjects and tell white lies and end up hating ourselves for not being truthful. With us it would be different, Mac. You don't have any hesitation about telling me what you really think—'

The small pager on his belt beeped insistently. He sighed and glanced at his watch, then went off to the telephone booth in the corner. When he came back, he didn't sit down; instead he propped a foot on his chair and said, 'As long as you're *persona non grata* around the apartment tonight, how would you like to be my insurance policy instead?'

'What?'

'That was Marguerite Gould. She's finally got around to looking at the property settlement Ridge Coltrain and I hashed out last week, and she wants me to come by and interpret it for her.'

'It was written in perfectly plain English,' Alisa objected.

'She's probably holding it upside down.' He picked up her bag and handed it to her.

She took a last, long swallow of coffee. 'We're in a hurry, I see. And what do you mean, insurance policy?'

'Last time I went to the house, she

was wearing a négligé that was mostly imagination trimmed in marabou, and she kept trying to ply me with martinis—'

'In that case, I can't think why you want to take me along.'

'Oh, I'm not worried about my honour,' he said airily. 'I'm sure you can picture Marguerite Gould in a négligé. But just in case her husband happens to still have the private detective watching her, and he threatens to tell the judge—'

'You want a witness who can testify that it was legal business and not monkey business going on. Sure, I'll come along. Why not?'

He rewarded her with a smile. 'You can sit in the corner and make meaningless pot-hooks on scrap paper and think about my reputation. If I had a wife, you know, my clients' husbands would be less suspicious—'

'And the clients would cause you less trouble? Now that's a fairy-tale, if ever I've heard one.'

'It couldn't hurt. And as long as you're thinking over my offer again—'

'Don't hold your breath, Justin.'

'Remember that it's not open indefinitely. I might run into the perfect woman at any moment.'

'And just what would the perfect woman see in you?' Alisa asked sweetly.

The million-watt smile flashed. 'That's exactly what I mean,' he pointed out. 'You wouldn't dare say that sort of thing to me if we were dating, Mac.'

Marguerite Gould had looked very disappointed when she'd flung the front door open and saw Alisa on the step, but it still took more than an hour to dispose of her questions. After that, Justin took Alisa to dinner at Emilio's. They quarrelled about national politics, tangled regarding the finer points of the First Amendment, and squabbled over the question of who really wrote the plays of William Shakespeare, but they agreed that Emilio had outdone himself in the kitchen.

'And after all,' Justin said, 'some issues are more important than others, and a good steak is right at the head of the list.'

As a result, it was late when he dropped her off at the apartment. The door of the extra bedroom was closed, and the living-room was dark and quiet. Vibrato raised his head from his perch atop the built-in china cabinet in the dining-room, then closed his eyes wearily. 'Poor kitty,' Alisa crooned softly. 'You're getting tired of constant company too, aren't you? All this confusion, and no safe place to curl up for a nap any more.'

The glass door that led on to the terrace opened with a soft slither just a couple of feet from her, and she jumped.

'You're late,' Clay said. 'I was worried.'

She refrained from telling him that it really wasn't his business any more to worry about her.

'It was silly of Shelley to make such a fuss, anyway,' he said. He sounded a little grumpy. 'There was no reason for you to make yourself scarce. Now that she's pregnant, Shelley's idea of celebrating has changed, you know.'

'I don't think this is something you should discuss with me, Clay.' She turned away, intending to go to her bedroom.

He clutched her elbow and spun her round. 'Why not?' he said hoarsely. 'You know how I feel, Alisa. And I know how tough it's been on you this week. You can't hide it from me, darling.' His mouth came down on hers, hard, violently seeking a response.

She twisted her face away from his. 'Clay—'

'I've made a horrible mistake,' he whispered. 'I need you, Alisa—'

'It's out of the question, Clay. You can't divorce her. She's your wife—she's carrying your child!'

'Shelley doesn't want to be a wife—she just wants to play house. All right, she can have her precious public image, her baby doll included. We can have each other anyway, Alisa. We won't even have to be careful. She's so wrapped up in herself that she'll never suspect a thing.'

For a long and timeless instant Alisa was motionless in his arms. His mouth, hot and demanding, pressed across her cheek, seeking her lips.

Then she said, calmly enough, 'Let me get this clear. No divorce?'

He scowled. 'Don't you start nagging me, too. Why give her everything I've worked for? I've slaved and sweated while she hasn't lifted a hand—'

'Shelley has always enjoyed having a good time,' she said quietly. 'But after all, Clay, that was what attracted you to her in the first place. I was too much of a spoil-sport for your taste. I was always thinking about tomorrow, and about how to pay for the good time.'

'You never were the life of the party,' he admitted. 'And she was a dazzler—'

'The truth is you want to have your cake and eat it, too, don't you, Clay? You want to have a woman at hand for whichever mood you happen to be in.'

He laughed. 'I probably shouldn't have said all that—sorry if I hurt your feelings. You think about it, darling, and when you decide to play along...'

And this is the man I thought I loved, she thought with a horrible, sickening clarity. The man I wanted to spend my life with—the man I wanted to share hearth and home and children with. The man I believed was my one perfect love...

'No, thanks,' she said curtly. Her voice was little more than a croak.

He laughed softly. 'Don't tell me you're not interested, Alisa. You love me.'

She shook her head violently.

Love, she thought. Perhaps Justin is right after all. All the trouble begins when people first think they're in love. Their judgement vanishes. They'd be much happier in the long run if they could just be sensible at the start. The truth is, love is nothing more than a myth, and the search for romance destroys lives. I've nearly let it destroy mine. Justin is right...

Clay tried to kiss her again, softly this time. She put an elbow firmly into the soft hollow just under his ribs. He jerked away with a muffled howl.

'Be careful,' Alisa warned. 'You'll wake your wife—and she might be very interested in this little scene.'

His face darkened with rage. 'And who do you think she'll believe? When I explain to her how you came on to me—'

'Go right ahead,' she said. 'But I think she'll listen to me.' She stopped for a second, and went on, very deliberately, more to herself than to him, 'And you'd better listen, too, Clay, before you open your mouth to Shelley and make trouble for yourself. Because, you see, I'm just not interested in you any more. I'm—I'm going to be married.'

CHAPTER SEVEN

For a moment, Alisa savoured the slack look of astonishment on Clay's face. Then she realised how vitally important it was that she talk to Justin right away. If she didn't, and Clay was waiting tomorrow morning when Justin came to pick her up...

Besides, she was half afraid she would suffocate if she stayed in the apartment. 'It's stifling in here, isn't it?' she said. 'I think I'll go out for some air.' She was fumbling in the side pocket of her handbag for her extra car keys as she ran down the steps outside. He hadn't said a word.

It was a beautiful night, with a nearly full moon lighting the desert, sending long, weird shadows across the still land. The miles went by swiftly, occupied by the swirling confusion of her thoughts, and she was startled when she found herself at the gateway to the small residential development. It looked different tonight in the harsh light; the houses almost vanished into the boulders and cacti that surrounded them, and the whole place had the eerie look of a lunar landscape.

Then a clean-cut young man in uniform stepped out of the guard shack and held up a hand. Alisa had forgotten that there would be a guard on duty here, no matter what the hour. And tonight it was not the friendly Roger who had been guarding the place the day Justin had brought her out here. This young man, she soon began to think, was heartless. If Mr Abernathy didn't know she was coming, then she could not go in. That was the rule.

'You could call him,' she suggested. 'It isn't quite midnight yet, and if I were you I wouldn't want to have to explain to him tomorrow why I turned away someone who was in the middle of an emergency.'

He looked at her for what seemed half a year. 'Your name?' he said finally.

She started to give it. Then she stopped

and wet her lips and said, 'Just tell him Mac needs to see him.'

He went into the guard shack, and she put her face down against the steering-wheel. Her head was spinning. If Justin isn't there, she thought, what will I do? But the guard would know if he hadn't come home yet. He has to be there...

In a couple of minutes the young man was back, standing very straight, acting very proper. He almost saluted, in fact. 'It's the third house on the—'

Alisa didn't wait for him to finish.

Justin opened the door before she had a chance to ring the bell. He was barefoot, wearing khaki walking shorts and a shirt that was open to the waist. The guard's call had obviously got him out of bed, Alisa concluded. His hair was rumpled as if he'd been running his hands through it. Or perhaps, she thought, as if someone else had...

'What brings you haring out here in the middle of the night, Mac?' He sounded curious, not cross.

It was a legitimate question, she thought.

It made her pause to think; she hadn't considered what she was going to say to him—or, perhaps even more important, what she wasn't going to say. How was she going to explain the suddenness of her decision—the importance that it be decided tonight?

She stepped past him into the hall; her heels clicked against the flagstone floor. She hadn't been in this part of the house last time; they'd come in the back way, through the kitchen. She could see a closed set of double doors towards the back of the house that must be the ones leading into the living-room. Opposite them, an identical set stood open. A dim light from the room beyond formed a pale puddle on the flagstones, and voices murmured indistinctly, punctuated by laughter, forming a pleasant, musical pattern.

'You have guests,' she said, feeling like a complete idiot.

'No. I was watching a new comedy act on television.'

The relief was incredible. 'Then you

haven't stumbled across the perfect woman this evening?'

'Why do I get the feeling this is a loaded question, Mac? All right—I'll bite. Not exactly—the lady I had dinner with isn't perfect at all. Is that the right answer?'

She swallowed hard. 'Well, I've been thinking it over, Justin, and I've decided you're right. About love, and—everything.'

There was a long and painful silence. 'Good God,' he said finally. 'The guard was right—this is an emergency. I think I need a belt of Scotch.' He pointed towards the lighted room. 'Make yourself at home.' He paused, as if the casual words had suddenly taken on a new meaning. Then he shook his head a little and went off towards the living-room.

'Make it two,' Alisa called after him.

He was gone for several minutes. She paced the long room—it was a library, and the dim light came from a dying fire as well as from the flickering television screen—and tried to think.

Should she tell him about Clay, about the sudden truth that had burst upon her tonight? Something deep inside her shuddered away from the idea; to Justin, who was so logical, so clear-thinking, the insanity of her belief that Clay had cared for her would be obvious. 'I'd look like a dunce,' she muttered, 'because I am one. I should have seen what Clay was from the beginning, and Justin won't hesitate to tell me that.'

And she didn't want to hear it from him. She didn't want him to know what a fool she had been. Now that her mad, quixotic longing for Clay was over, what was the point in telling Justin? It was all history now—perhaps not exactly ancient, but certainly past, and she didn't want to be another Desirée Coltrain, telling him the details of her past loves. If she was actually going to marry him, perhaps it would be better to keep it to herself.

If, she reminded herself. When it came right down to it, he hadn't sounded very enthusiastic about the idea.

She straightened her shoulders as he came back into the room with two glasses. He turned off the television set in the corner and waved her towards a leather couch. 'Sorry,' he said. 'That wasn't a very gentlemanly way to receive the news that you've accepted my proposal, was it?'

The glass of Scotch was cold in her hand. 'Well, I'm not sure I have, exactly,' she began. 'I mean—I was thinking, and wouldn't it be just as effective if we simply pretended to be engaged for a while? That would surely discourage Debbie, and it would also let Clay and Shelley know that they can't sponge off me forever.'

But it wouldn't make them get out of my apartment, she thought. It wouldn't get me away from Clay entirely.

She could almost see him turning the idea over in his head, examining it from every side. 'But it doesn't answer any of the problems in the long run,' he pointed out. 'And it really isn't what you came out here to do. Is it, Alisa?'

'No,' she whispered. 'It isn't. But—'

'But you thought I was looking for a way out? That you'd accidentally called my bluff?' He shook his head. 'I'm not playing games. And neither should you. If you agree to this, be certain it's what you truly want—and that you're going to feel the same way next week, and ten years from now.'

'Because changing my mind is not an option,' she said. 'That goes for you, too, Justin.'

'I mean what I've said—every word of it.' He leaned against the ivory bricks of the big fireplace, his drink lazily cupped in the palm of his hand. 'I enjoy your company; you enjoy mine. We don't agree on everything, but that will keep things interesting. The crucial point is that we see the really vital things the same way—the importance of family, the value of permanent commitment, the fleeting nature of what people call love. We'll have something which is a lot more lasting than that—we'll have trust, and honesty, and understanding. What better alternative is there?'

It was all so logical, so clear-headed, so reasonable. If love had flown forever out of the window—and it had, she was honest enough to admit that; if she could be so badly mistaken about Clay, how could she ever again put her trust in the illogical thing called falling in love?—then why not seize the best that was available to her, and be happy with it?

She looked around at the untidy library, its shadowed shelves half empty, and thought of her own small apartment, with the few brave personal touches she had added. She had tried for a year to pretend that it was a home, and she was tired of trying.

I want a real home, she thought. I want a family. I won't ever feel the ecstasy for Justin that every woman wants to feel, that every woman dreams she'll find with her husband. But trust, and honesty, and understanding—those things might be more important, in the long run...

She looked up at him. The dimming fire cast long fingers of light across the room, and his face was shadowed. But she didn't need to see it to remember. In a profession that had lost public trust because of shady operators and corrupt deals, Justin Abernathy was universally well respected. No one had ever doubted his word; no one had ever questioned his ethics... His wife would never have reason to suspect him.

'Yes,' she said. It was only a breath, and even in the almost-silence of the room she wondered for an instant if she had said it at all.

He was still for a long instant, and then he set his glass aside and came across the room to sit beside her. 'Thank you,' he said, and reached for her hand, drawing the back of it up to his lips.

She leaned against him with a weary little sigh, and for a long time they sat that way, silent, watching the dying fire. She wondered a little what he might be thinking. Her own thoughts were a sort of tired little abstract pattern in her brain.

'There's one thing we haven't really talked about,' she said finally. 'And perhaps we should. You said, I think, that sexual compatibility wasn't the only important thing, but—'

'Of course I expect that making love will be an enjoyable part of our lives. I don't think you need to be frightened, my dear—'

It was so gentle that suddenly she couldn't stand it any more. She interrupted, almost harshly. 'I'm not a virgin, Justin.'

His eyebrows lifted slightly. 'Well, I'm sorry if it disappoints you, Mac,' he said drily, 'but neither am I. I have no intention of describing my experience, because it isn't relevant. And I have only one question for you...'

She braced herself a little. I cannot lie to him, she reminded herself. But there are truths that I would much rather not tell...

'Was making love unpleasant for you?'

She was startled. 'No—no, it wasn't.'

'Then I think that it will take care of itself, given a little time.' He turned her face up to his and kissed her, and she let her eyelids drift shut and tried to think of nothing at all.

It was a very gentle kiss, with no demands. It was more of an exploration, she thought a little hazily, the beginning of a new adventure. It was very pleasant, really, and she was a little surprised when he said firmly, 'It's late. And you're tired. I don't think you should drive all the way home. I'll take you, if you like—'

She shook her head. 'Then it would be even later when you got to bed.' But she didn't move.

'Right. So why don't you stay here?'

Her eyes snapped open, and Justin laughed ruefully. 'This is not a pass, it's common sense.' He tugged her to her feet. 'Just let me get some things out of my bedroom.'

She followed him, a bit reluctantly. There was yet another hallway leading back through yet another wing. She lost count of doors. Surely they couldn't all be bedrooms...?

I'm going to need a ball of string to find my way around, she mused.

At the end of the hall lay a big suite. She caught a glimpse of a marble-walled bathroom off to one side, and then he led her through a big dressing-room lined with storage cupboards and into a bedroom that filled the entire width of the wing. There were windows on two sides, and at the back were a pair of glass doors that had to lead out towards the pool. There were no curtains, just blinds, and the big bed had neither headboard nor bedspread, just bright plaid sheets and a blanket neatly folded at the foot.

He took a robe down from a hook on the back of the door and said, 'I'll be on the couch in the library if you need anything.'

'Why?'

'I told you earlier—there's no furniture in the other bedrooms,' he explained. 'Did you think I was just making excuses for not adopting your house guests?'

A delicate pink flush coloured her cheeks. 'That wasn't what I meant, exactly.'

He looked her over. 'Then what did you mean—exactly?'

She took a deep breath. 'It just seems sort of silly. I mean, it's a perfectly big bed—'

'Are you suggesting we just draw a line down the middle of it?'

'No,' she whispered. She didn't look at him, but at her clasped hands. 'Not at all.'

He looked at her for a long moment, and then he smiled, a particularly tender smile. 'You don't have to go to bed with me tonight, you know. Making love is not a test you have to pass.'

No, she thought. It's more like putting a sizeable down payment on a condominium —it means you're committed and can't change your mind about moving.

'Making love isn't a skill that you either have or don't have,' Justin went on. 'It develops as two people learn to trust each other. We can't expect to have that yet, Alisa.'

'But we have to start somewhere, don't we? Somewhere—and some time.'

For the space of a breath the room was silent.

A wave of colour seemed to start in the pit of her stomach and sweep upwards until her face was burning. 'If you don't want to, Justin, I understand.'

Soft-footed, he came across the carpet

to her, and took her into, his arms. 'That is not the problem,' he said, and kissed her.

There was nothing tentative about the way his mouth caressed hers, nothing hesitant about the way his hands slipped down over her back to cup her hipbones and hold her close against him. His tongue slipped gently between her lips, and the tension inside her seemed to uncurl its hold and drain slowly away.

'I am not a saint,' he whispered against her mouth. 'And you could tempt any number of them...'

It was a lovely lie, she thought. She almost reminded him that they had promised each other truth, and nothing else. But before she could frame the words he was kissing her again. The empty spot inside her where the fear had been began to slowly fill with anticipation.

Her dress slipped to the carpet almost unheeded, except for the feeling of freedom that its absence left her. When he disposed of her bra, she savoured the tingling sensation of the hair on his chest as it rubbed against her soft breasts. And when he put her down on the bed and bent to take one delicate nipple into his mouth, she writhed and locked her hands together at the back of his neck and pulled him down to her.

'There's no hurry,' he said, but he sounded a little breathless; self-control was already slipping away.

In the last coherent moment before chaos overwhelmed her, Alisa thought, Different—that's all. But an instant later she could not remember what she was comparing with this supremely satisfying, soul-shaking sensation. In any case, it didn't matter. All that was important just now was the two of them, and the incredible beauty she had caught sight of, just a little distance away...

It was more than beautiful, and after it was over she basked in the glory of it, unwilling to stir and take the chance of shattering that iridescent memory. It might have been mere minutes, or an hour, before Justin sighed and turned his head until his lips brushed the satin hollow at the base of her throat, and said huskily, 'Mac?'

She murmured something indistinct.

'Perhaps it won't take as much time as I thought.'

She smiled a little, and slid wearily down into exhausted slumber. It was probably fortunate that she was too tired to dream.

It was early when they reached her apartment but Alisa had barely inserted her key into the dead-bolt lock when she heard the quarrel raging inside. Shelley was screaming something about the police; Clay's deeper, calmer voice said, 'She'll come back when she's good and ready. She's an adult, after all.'

Alisa looked up at Justin and bit her lip. He reached over her shoulder and pushed the door open. Shelley wheeled around; the relief that flooded her face was almost instantly replaced by fury. 'Where have you been?' she shrieked. 'Scaring us to death like this—'

'At the Pancake House,' Justin said innocently. 'Having breakfast.'

Clay's eyes narrowed, but he didn't say anything.

'All night?' Shelley spat. 'It's rather obvious what you've been up to—that's the same dress you were wearing yesterday, Alisa. You could have called and said you weren't coming home, at least!'

So Clay didn't tell her that I was at home for a while, Alisa thought.

'Clay's right, Shelley. Your sister is an adult.' Justin brought Alisa's hand casually up to his face and rubbed it against his jaw. 'Don't you think we'd better tell them, Alisa?'

She swallowed hard and looked up at him longingly. She was terrified that she would trip over her own tongue; it had seemed such a simple, plausible story when they'd planned it out over blueberry pancakes, but now that she was actually facing this virago of a sister—to say nothing of Clay—it didn't seem so easy. She hadn't planned on facing them both so early this morning...

'We weren't going to say anything at all, you see,' Justin confided. 'We intended the ceremony to be very private, with no guests at all, so when you came, rather than explain it all, we just postponed everything. But of course it's no use trying to keep it secret any more, is it?'

'Ceremony?' Shelley said blankly. 'You mean—you're getting married?'

Justin didn't bother to answer. He looked down at Alisa instead. 'Remind me to get your engagement ring out of the bank vault today, darling.'

She blinked, and said feebly, 'Of course, Justin.' Engagement ring? Bank vault? That was a new embellishment to the story. If he ever decides to stop practising law, she thought, he can probably write one heck of a mystery novel.

Blandly, he added to Shelley, 'It's been driving her crazy to be without it, poor girl, but of course she couldn't wear it this week without raising all sorts of suspicions.'

Clay gave a snort. 'When is the wedding, Alisa?' There was a nasty twist to his voice.

Justin was the one who answered. 'It was originally set for this weekend, and now that we've accidentally let the cat out of the bag I suppose we might as well go back to our original plans.'

'Why, you little devil,' Shelley said. 'I knew there was something wrong, Alisa—something unusual—but I never dreamed it was anything like this.' She swept across the room and engulfed her sister in a hug. 'I'm so happy for you, but I could shake you for not telling me!'

It worked, Alisa thought. It actually worked!

She didn't realise until much later, when she was at the office and nearly finished with the mail, how closely she had been treading to disaster in the last week. 'I knew there was something wrong,' Shelley had said. Now she would never have a reason to wonder if something altogether different might have been the cause of Alisa's preoccupation.

Bless you, Justin, she thought, with a catch in her throat. You've got me off the hook completely, and you don't even know it.

It was shortly after that when a short,

plump man wearing an old-fashioned suit, a diamond tie-pin and a toupee came quietly into her office, carrying an attaché case. 'Mr Abernathy is expecting me,' he said briskly.

That's news to me, Alisa thought. 'Mr Abernathy is with a client at the moment.'

He gave her a gold-toothed smile. 'I'll be happy to wait.' He sat down across the room from her, the attaché case arranged squarely on his lap, his hands folded motionless atop it, as if he was prepared to sit there for weeks.

Alisa put her glasses back on and picked up the next envelope, a heavyweight ivory bond engraved with Louise Abernathy's initials. 'Dear Miss McClenaghan,' the letter began, 'Since your manners are infinitely better than those of my great-nephew, I've decided to stop writing to him altogether...'

I wonder how Louise is going to take the news, Alisa thought. Will she give me a grand welcome, or are mere good manners enough of a recommendation for entry into the family? And just how does Justin plan to break it to her? Via car telephone, on his way to the judge's office?

Justin's door opened and the new client left. 'Gerard!' Justin said cheerfully from the threshold. 'Thanks for coming on such short notice.'

The prim man with the attaché case vanished into the inside office. Five minutes later, the intercom summoned Alisa; she picked up her notebook and went in.'

Justin was sitting on the corner of his desk, and scattered over the top of it were half a dozen black-velvet-lined trays, each studded with rings that sparkled and glittered in the glow of the desk lamp.

Alisa's eyes widened at the display, but she kept her voice carefully casual. 'This is only part of the contents of your bank vault, I'm sure, Justin?'

The brilliance of his smile was dimmed only slightly by comparison with the stones. 'I was rather proud of that,' he admitted. 'It occurred to me that I'd better say something fast, or Shelley would expect you to dig your engagement ring out of a bottom drawer somewhere and show it to her right then. What would you like, Mac? Pick a ring—any ring.'

'You sound like a carnival barker.' She moved a little closer. There had to be fifty rings on the desk, spread out in a shimmering rainbow of colour.

'That was what I wanted to be when I was five. I like this one, myself. Look at all the flash.' He plucked a large diamond from the tray and turned it under the light.

The prim little man smiled and said gently, *'Fire,* Mr Abernathy, is the generally accepted term. Not *flash.'*

Alisa wasn't listening. She let her gaze slide across the rows of gems. They were all more like dress rings than the small solitaire diamond and plain band she had expected. They were beautiful, of course—any woman would give her soul to own a ring like that—but they were also so obviously expensive that it made her shudder inside. It didn't feel right somehow to let Justin spend that sort of money on a ring.

She picked up one that contained a

deep blue stone surrounded by icy white diamonds set in platinum. It was beautiful, and surely a sapphire, even such a large one, would be less expensive...?

'A fine choice,' the jeweller said, beaming. 'It's rare to find a perfect diamond in that shade of blue.'

Alisa put it down hastily. When, five minutes later, she had not picked up another ring, Justin was beginning to frown.

Just close your eyes and reach for one, she told herself. It doesn't matter, really.

But it did. There was one that had drawn her eye the instant she had walked in...

It was a rich green gem cut in an oval, surrounded by small diamonds, and mounted on a broad band that was woven of gold wire. It was delicate and lacy and beautiful.

But the stone was twice as big as the blue diamond, and she was afraid to pick the ring up—afraid of what it would turn out to be, and even more afraid that once she held it in her hand she would not be able to put it down. It looked so very right—and surely it couldn't hurt to ask? She pointed at it. 'Is that an emerald?'

'That is a tsavorite garnet,' the jeweller said. 'Even more beautiful than an emerald in colour, I've always thought. That particular stone is extremely well cut; notice the lovely way it catches the light. Would you like to try it on?'

A garnet, she thought, and nodded. The ring slipped securely on to her slim finger and nestled there.

Justin shifted on the corner of the desk. 'Dammit, Mac, don't you want a really stunning, knock-your-eyes-out diamond? This one, perhaps—?'

'No.' She swallowed hard and tried to soften it. 'Please, Justin. Can't I have something less elaborate? Something I can wear all the time and not have to worry about?'

He looked at her for a long moment. Then he reached out and took her hand, where the garnet glowed softly green against her fair skin, and drew her close to the desk, till she was standing between his knees with his arm around her.

'It's an honest ring,' she whispered. 'It doesn't pretend to be what it isn't.'

He looked at the ring, and then at her face, just on a level with his. 'It's also the colour of your eyes when you're being particularly stubborn,' he mused. 'I suppose that alone makes it the perfect choice. All right, Mac. You win.'

She smiled and kissed him softly. 'Thank you, Justin.'

His arm tightened until she was leaning against him, slightly off balance. 'And it even fits, too,' he murmured.

The jeweller cleared his throat. 'And what about the wedding ring?' he asked gently.

The gleam in Justin's eyes dared Alisa to object. 'Use your best judgement, Gerard.'

'I shall, Mr Abernathy,' the jeweller said primly. He lifted the attaché case to the desk and opened it; from inside came the dull gleam of more stones.

'What are those?' Alisa asked.

Justin said, sounding a little pained, 'Please don't tell me you want to start over again, Mac.'

The jeweller suppressed a smile. 'Mr Abernathy felt that those rings were not worthy to take a place on your hand, Miss Mac,' he said diplomatically. 'And I agreed. A lovely hand like yours should be graced with a stone of rare beauty—the kind that Mr Abernathy has an eye for. I'll have the wedding ring ready this afternoon.'

When he was gone, Alisa stared into the depths of the tsavorite garnet for a long while, and then said, 'Justin, how much is this thing going to cost you?'

He stopped dialling a telephone number and said plaintively, 'Mac, if you're going to turn into a mercenary little wretch—'

'I'm not! You know why I'm asking. Is it less than the diamonds, or not?'

He slammed the telephone down. 'Do you like the ring, or don't you?'

'I love it!' She drew a long, shaky breath. 'But—'

'Then it doesn't matter whether it costs

twice what the diamonds did, or half as much, does it?'

'But you know I didn't intend—I don't want you to think I set out to—'

'What you really mean is that you intended to choose the least expensive ring in the tray, didn't you? Well, you didn't succeed, and if you think I'm going to call Gerard back here so you can compare prices, you're wrong, Mac! It doesn't matter a tinker's damn to me what the thing costs!'

She burst into tears, and he swore under his breath and came across the room to put his arms around her. 'I'm sorry, darling,' he said. 'But I thought you might do something like that, which is why I told him to put half the stuff away where you couldn't see it and take the price-tags off the rest.'

'I just thought—' She began to sob.

'That because I'm not in love with you and you're not in love with me, any kind of a ring is unnecessary and an expensive one is foolish, is that it?' He pushed her a tiny distance away from him, his hands firm on her shoulders. 'As if our being honest somehow makes this whole thing second-rate! Dammit, Mac, get that notion out of your head right now. We aren't going to cut corners and cheat ourselves—and if I want to give you one of those diamond dress rings for Christmas then you'd better smile and say thank you, even if you have to spend the next eight months practising—'

'Justin,' she said weakly, 'you're shaking me.

He swore under his breath and pulled her against him again, so tightly that she could hardly breathe. She hadn't realised that breathing had gone out of style, she thought dizzily a few moments later, in the midst of the most devastating kiss she had ever experienced. It was funny, though; she didn't miss it a bit.

CHAPTER EIGHT

The judge who was to marry them in his chambers that evening made a few gentle wisecracks about the unexpectedness of the situation before he disappeared into his office to put on his robes and his official personality. Alisa was not surprised by the quips, and Justin was amused; even in a city the size of Phoenix a limited number of people spent all their time on divorces, and they all knew each other well. As Justin said, it would be a wonder if a few wisecracks were all they had to suffer.

But the judge's humour didn't help the case of nervous butterflies that threatened to overwhelm her. She tried to hide it, but Justin caught her sneaking deep breaths, and said, 'It's only a formality, you know. As far as I'm concerned, we made our vows to each other last night.'

She smiled, a little.

'And not in the bedroom, either,' he said, sounding a little cross. 'Before that. A complete and lifelong commitment, Alisa. No looking back, no wondering.'

If I didn't know better, she thought, I'd say he sounds like a romantic...

It was a brief, simple, beautiful ceremony. The judge had some wise and thoughtful things to say about the multitudes of wrecked marriages they had all seen, and how love was not enough to assure their own success. Justin's hand closed firmly over Alisa's trembling fingers, as if to express his complete agreement, and he didn't let go until it was time to retrieve her wedding ring from his waistcoat pocket.

He had reclaimed the tsavorite garnet on the way to the judge's chambers; now, as they left the building, he slipped it back on her finger with a flourish. There was an extra sparkle attached; she sneaked a look at it and realised that now there was a narrow row of diamonds circling her finger below the braided band and a second identical row above, to act as a sort of guard for the engagement ring. Was this a sample of the jeweller's good judgement, she wondered, or had he been reading Justin's mind? It was beautiful, there was no question about that. The icy fire of the perfectly matched diamonds was the ideal foil for the glowing green warmth of the tsavorite garnet.

She told Justin so, meekly, as they ate chateaubriand in a very small, very quiet restaurant. He hesitated a second, as if expecting that a protest would inevitably follow the compliment, and when she remained silent he told her that he was proud of her for learning so swiftly how to accept a gift.

'Does this mean I can expect a shower of this sort of thing?' she asked. 'Because I'd much rather have the money to hire a decorator and buy some furniture and wallpaper and—'

He frowned at the strawberry tart the waitress had just set in front of him. 'Can't you just do it yourself? Decorators always want to put ruffles on everything.' He stabbed a strawberry and offered it to her.

'Didn't we have a discussion about trust, Justin?' She nibbled the berry delicately; it was the sweetest one she had ever tasted. 'I promise I'm not going to do anything that's in bad taste. That's why I want a decorator.'

He gave a disbelieving snort.

She ignored him. 'Besides, I'll have to wait till my furniture arrives from Green Bay, and then we can decide what else we need.'

'What kind of furniture?'

'I inherited some of the things from my grandmother. Others I picked up at auctions and shops—you know, like the fern stand I'm refinishing.'

That seemed to cheer him up a bit. 'I like the stuff that's in your apartment,' he offered.

'That's great, Justin,' she said with irony. 'But most of that—fortunately—doesn't belong to me. All of my stuff is stacked in Jeff Winslow's basement in Green Bay—'

'All?' he interrupted. 'How much stuff are we talking about?'

'A small truckload—certainly not a

houseful. And I called Jeff today and told him to ship it as soon as possible, so it's a little too late to change my mind about bringing it down here.'

'I wouldn't dare try. Wonderful things to have, ex-bosses,' he murmured. 'They come in so handy for little favours like this.'

'And now I'm acquiring another one,' Alisa said. 'Ex-boss, that is. Jeff wanted to know what on earth I was thinking of to marry you. He seems to think you're a terrible risk.'

He laughed and told her a couple of slightly malicious stories about Jeff and their law-school days, and she thought he'd forgotten all about the decorator. But when they got home and he went to the little bar to open a bottle of champagne he looked around the lofty-ceilinged living-room and admitted, 'I suppose it could stand a little work.'

Alisa bit her tongue. Honesty was a virtue, she told herself, but diplomacy would obviously get her further in the long run.

Justin handed her a tulip-shaped glass, lit the fire and drew her down on the love-seat beside him, and in a matter of minutes things like furniture had slipped from her mind entirely, as desire began to whisper instructions to her dazed brain.

It might have been just a day since the first time they had made love, but what she felt with him was an eerie combination of anticipation and familiarity, as if he had always been her lover, as if her body knew from long experience precisely how to react to give them both the supreme pleasure they sought. Yet she also knew that there were wonderful things still to be explored—enough wonderful things to fill a lifetime...

The champagne was forgotten; it was unimportant compared to the exhilarating, drugging impact of his kisses. He undressed her slowly by firelight, and each movement of his hands was in itself a slow seduction, until she was whimpering, begging—almost sobbing with the agony of wanting him—as they made love on the hearthrug with the crackling flames providing the only light and the only background music they needed.

Afterwards, he moved to stir the fire, and lay quietly, staring into it. He didn't pull her close against him to revel in the afterglow of lovemaking, and she was vaguely disappointed. She tried to laugh at herself, because snuggling into his arms last night had been like nestling down into a warm, soft, secure blanket, she had already come to expect that the brief time after making love would always be as wonderful as it had been then.

She sat up and reached for her glass of champagne. It had gone flat, and that only added to her dissatisfaction. A few minutes ago, she thought, everything had been so perfect. The two of them, in each other's arms, experiencing together such a burst of pleasure that she had screamed his name—

The champagne glass tipped in her nerveless hand, and the wine quietly trickled out, forming a pale gold pool on the plush carpet.

She didn't see the mess it made, for

she had squeezed her eyelids tight in an attempt to abolish the horrible memory that was ringing through her head. But she could not shut off the sound that echoed through her mind—the sound of what she had said. It was like a crackly old recording running at the wrong speed, but there was no doubt that it was her voice.

And in that moment of supreme joy it had not been Justin's name she had called out. It had been Clay's.

It was long minutes later before she even dared to look at him. He was still stretched out on the hearthrug, his chin propped on his hands, staring into the fire.

'Justin,' she said. Her voice was hoarse. 'Is there any way I can tell you how sorry I am?'

He didn't move, didn't even turn his head. 'It's all right to pretend that I'm Clay, Alisa,' he said quietly. 'Just remember that nothing more than pretending is allowed.'

It was calm, so matter of fact that she wanted to throw herself on him and pound her fists against his chest and force him to admit the anger he felt—the anger he must feel. When a woman lying in his arms in the throes of passion sobbed out another man's name, it had to wound his pride, if nothing more, and make him want to strike out at her...

Not if love doesn't come into it, she thought.

I'm back to that again, she told herself hopelessly. How deeply ingrained are my expectations of how married couples should behave! But in this situation all bets are off, she reminded herself. Justin has written his own set of rules.

But her heart would not accept that explanation. He could not be so cold that this did not matter, she thought. It might be part of the past, but it had to have been a shock, no matter what—

That explains it, she thought. It wasn't a shock. That's why he's so deadly calm about it.

'You weren't surprised,' she said quietly. 'You knew. Even before this happened, you knew.'

He sighed. 'It wasn't hard to guess.'

'How?'

For a moment she thought he wasn't going to answer. 'The way you looked at him,' he said finally. 'Let it go, Alisa. Please.'

But she couldn't. 'Doesn't it bother you? That I slept with the man who's my sister's husband? I never did—I swear it—after they were married.' Her voice was taut.

'I trust your word, Alisa. You don't have to give me the details.' He still hadn't looked at her.

She swallowed hard. 'I didn't intend to say anything, because I know you don't want to hear it,' she whispered. 'But now—I need to tell you, Justin.'

'The past is not important.'

'But you also said we need to have truth between us. And the truth is that I'm afraid. If you don't know what really happened, then you might believe it was worse than it was.'

He didn't answer. But he didn't get up and walk away, either, and she took a tight grip on her courage and stared at her hands, where the knuckles showed white, and started to talk in a low and expressionless voice.

'Clay and I never actually lived together. I don't know why we didn't, really,' she said, almost to herself. 'Perhaps he was keeping his options open. No, that isn't fair. I don't want to make him sound like a villain—we weren't actually engaged. We had sort of an unspoken understanding, that's all... At any rate, a year ago when Shelley came to visit me for a few weeks I didn't tell her to keep her hands off Clay; I didn't think there was any need.'

He sighed. 'And what if you had told her?' He sounded tired, but resigned, as if he knew there was no way to stop her.

'You mean, would she have gone after him anyway? I don't think so, Justin. You haven't seen Shelley at her best—'

'I should hope this isn't her best.'

'But she isn't like that, really. She isn't vindictive.'

'She wouldn't try to take a man away from you out of jealousy—just to prove she could?'

'Of course not. She isn't the sort to be jealous—and what reason would she have to be jealous of me, anyway? They fell in love, and they eloped, that's all. She had no idea that Clay and I— She still doesn't. And she won't.' Her voice was vehement.

Justin looked at her almost sadly. 'That marriage is doomed, you know.'

'Perhaps it is.' It made her sad to think about it, but she had to admit that he was probably right.

'I've never seen two people who were so immature, insincere, and selfish—'

'Nevertheless, if my sister's marriage blows apart,' Alisa said slowly, 'I don't want to be at the centre of it.'

'A laudable sentiment.' His voice was dry.

'I've seen too much of that sort of thing. My parents' marriage was in shreds even before I was born, I think. My first memory is of their fights—my mother crying, and my father storming off and not coming back for days sometimes.'

He stirred a little. 'Alisa—'

'I know, now, that my mother must

227

have already chosen her second husband by the time the divorce was final. I don't mean to criticise her for it, exactly—it wouldn't have been easy to make her way alone with a small child. She chose a man who was as unlike my father as any man could be, I think. Matthew Rhodes was—is—very dependable, very straightforward. Very rigid.'

He had turned his head; he was watching her.

'I don't mean that he mistreated me—he didn't. But the rules were the rules, and there was no arguing with them. At least, not for me. For Shelley—his own daughter—well, that was a different story.'

She thought she heard him say, 'It often is,' and she held her breath for an instant. But he didn't go on—if, indeed, he had really said anything at all.

'My father was like so many of the men we have to search out and force to pay their child-care obligations,' she went on quietly. 'After the first few months he didn't come to pick me up for visits any more, and he stopped sending money, too. Matt took over the financial responsibility, and I never exactly went without anything, but I heard him complain sometimes to my mother about it. And I soon learned that if there was something I wanted, the best way to get it was to convince Shelley she wanted it—because when she asked for it, he'd sometimes buy two. And even if he didn't, she would share. Shelley was always generous with her toys.'

'Somehow I doubt she would include Clay in that category,' he observed drily. 'She might not be the jealous sort, but—'

She made a hopeless little gesture, and tried to go on, but her throat was too tight.

'I'm sorry, Alisa.' It was no more than a breath.

After a painful little pause, she said, 'Matt always provided the things I needed, but it wasn't the same as having my own father. I hated to ask for anything—I hated depending on him. Shelley was all sunshine and laughter—she could charm him into doing anything, and he loved to do things for her. I was the troublesome child, the reminder that Mother hadn't always been his wife.' She stopped, and a moment later said, 'Then my mother died, and as soon as I was old enough I got an after-school job, and I started buying my own things whenever I could, so I didn't have to ask him for anything. I put myself through business college, I moved to Green Bay and went to work for Jeff, and I met Clay...'

Her voice trailed off. She had come full circle; there was nothing else to say.

He reached for the poker and jabbed it into the fire; a log snapped into fragments, and a shower of sparks sailed up the chimney. 'What was it that brought you out here in such a tearing hurry last night, Alisa? What made you change your mind?'

She swallowed hard. She should have expected he would ask, and there was no option she could see but to tell the truth. 'Last night,' she said deliberately, 'Clay suggested that we simply pick up our affair behind Shelley's back.'

'So that's why you married me.' He didn't really sound interested. 'To protect Clay.' He had turned back to stare into the fire.

'No!' She felt a little sick at the idea. 'Justin, you can't think I would do that—marry you to protect myself while I carried on an affair!'

'That's not quite what I said, Alisa. There won't be an affair. You've given me your solemn promise, and I don't believe you'd go back on it. Nevertheless, you are still protecting Clay, and yourself—'

She shook her head violently. 'It's not that. I don't know why I didn't just tell him to get out last night.' Her eyes were dark pools in the dim light. 'It was the middle of the night, and Shelley—'

'So your intention was to protect Shelley?'

'I suppose it was. I would have had to explain it if I'd thrown him out, and it would have been horrible.' She wet her lips. 'I'm sorry, Justin. You're right. That's one hell of a reason for marrying you, isn't it?'

231

There was a long silence, and then he said, so softly that she almost wondered if he had spoken at all, 'Is that the only reason?'

She shook her head slowly. 'No. I feel safe with you. Even now—after I've told you all this—I feel safe. I know it sounds like a contradiction, but even if you would tell me right now to get out—'

'Don't be a fool, Alisa.' It was almost sharp. 'Nothing has changed. It's over, and we're going to forget it.' He scattered the remaining remnants of the fire and watched till the flames had burned down to glowing embers. 'It's late. Let's get some sleep.'

She closed her eyes for a moment in thankful silence. Until that instant, she had not realised how much she had feared that the confession she had forced on his unwilling ears would bring everything tumbling down around her.

She moved quietly around the bedroom suite. He watched as she washed her face, so intently that it made her nervous. He was observing her so closely that she found herself wondering if he could read her mind.

When she finally asked him, he smiled a little and said, 'No. It's the soap—I thought women stopped using that stuff years ago. Why? Are you thinking something I should know about?'

As if none of it was important, she thought. And perhaps it wasn't, to him. He had known about Clay all the time, so of course it didn't change anything. And as for the rest—he had also seemed to understand how important it had been for her to tell him what had happened, but now he had put that, too, out of his mind. It was over, he had said. It didn't matter to them any more. It should be forgotten altogether.

She dug into the small suitcase that lay open on one wide window-seat and pulled a filmy cotton nightgown out. There hadn't been time to do more than pack a single case today. 'I'll have to get the rest of my clothes from the apartment some time this weekend,' she said, almost tentatively.

'And the cat, of course. Shelley said she'd feed him, but—'

Justin took the gown out of her hands, draped it across the suitcase, and turned her into his arms. The warmth of his body was reassuring, and she relaxed against him with a sigh, putting her head down against his shoulder. He was so strong, so dependable, she thought. He did understand, after all...

He pulled her down on to the bed with him, her body sprawled across his. She reached for the switch on the bedside lamp, but before she could extinguish the light his fingertips slid softly from her shoulders down the length of her arms. With one hand, he pinned both of her wrists against the pillow above his head, holding her gently prisoner and leaving his other hand free to explore the sensual secrets of her body. The only way she could move was to wriggle against him.

'You know what it's like,' she said suddenly. 'It's not just general empathy you feel—you know what it's like to lose a parent, don't you?'

'Let's not discuss it just now, Mac.' It was husky, but it was unmistakably an order. At any rate, she had no desire to press the subject; the sensations he was arousing were far more interesting.

But much later, when she was curled against him like a contented kitten, basking in the dim pool of light from the bedside lamps, listening with fascination to the slowing beat of his heart under her ear, she broached the subject again. 'Were your parents divorced, Justin?'

He released a long breath. 'Yes,' he said quietly. 'It was different from your situation, of course—I wasn't abandoned, but I can tell you all about how it feels to be the rope in a tug of war.'

'A custody battle?'

He nodded, and his chin brushed her hair. 'Sometimes I thought neither of them really wanted me at all, that the main goal was to hurt the other one.'

She held her breath for a moment, hoping that he would go on.

But he seemed to think better of it, and his voice grew almost stern. 'Let's skip the

235

details, all right? Both my parents are dead now. None of that matters any more.'

She didn't need the details; she could imagine them. She had seen psychological warfare waged by unhappy people who tried to brainwash their children into believing the other parent was a villain. And she could understand why he didn't want to talk about it.

Some day he will, she told herself. And in the meantime—well, it was very clear now why he had the attitude he did about love, and commitment, and promises.

As if he had heard her thoughts, he whispered, 'The only thing that matters is that it won't happen to our children, Mac.'

She shook her head and tried to fight off a yawn, and didn't succeed. A little corner of her heart grew warm at the thought of children, but she didn't feel quite comfortable yet discussing it. Instead, she murmured, 'My name isn't Mac any more, you know,' and went to sleep before there was an answer.

When Alisa woke on Saturday morning, Justin was not beside her, and she was half-afraid for a moment, remembering the night before. Even after she was fully awake, it took all of her courage to find her terry bathrobe in the bottom of her suitcase and pad through the house looking for him.

Don't be such a fool, she lectured herself. If he was going to walk out on you, he'd have done it last night instead of taking you to bed.

The master bedroom had been dark, the windows shaded, and it had fooled her into thinking that it was still very early. But in the rest of the house sunshine was streaming brightly across carpets, across flagstones, across polished wood floors. The warm patterns it created against the texture of wood and stone and textiles were beautiful, and yet sad—the emptiness of the house tugged at her heart.

It won't take long, she told herself. Clean out all the dust and bring in some good furnishings. Then give it a little time to acquire some personality, and it will quickly become a home instead of an empty hotel lobby.

Justin was not in the library, and there was no evidence that he had been there. The living-room was just as they had left it the previous night. She realised that the doors of the sun-porch, beyond the living-room, stood open to the warm breeze, and just then a splash drew her attention to the pool, where Justin was methodically swimming laps. He pulled himself up to the edge as she came across the tiled patio, and his smile almost rocked her off her feet. 'I wondered if you were planning to sleep all day,' he teased. 'Come on in—it'll wake you up, lazybones.'

'I don't have a suit on.'

'Who's going to see?' He waved a dripping hand at the high wall that surrounded the property. Here it was solid, without the occasional wrought-iron panels that decorated the front of the house. And he was right; the way the houses had been arranged in this little development, they might as well have been out in the middle of the desert, without a neighbour for miles.

So she dropped her terry robe in a heap on the side of the pool and discovered what a luxurious feeling it was to slide through the water without even a wispy bikini to impede her progress.

Sheer luxury, she thought finally, as she pulled herself out of the water and stretched out in a lounge chair beside the pool to enjoy the sunshine.

Justin followed her. He perched on the arm of her chair and used a lock of her wet hair to trace her profile. 'What does a guy have to do around here to get breakfast?'

She didn't open her eyes. 'Depends. Is there anything in the refrigerator?'

A bell mounted beside the porch door shrilled, and Alisa jumped a foot.

'It's just the telephone,' Justin said. 'I'm amazed it's been quiet this long, though I had sort of hoped all my clients would conspire to have a peaceful weekend.'

'Were you always such an idealistic dreamer?'

He made a face at her, shrugged into his robe and went to answer it.

Alisa was lying there, thinking about

going to rummage in the kitchen for the makings of an omelette, when he came back. 'Don't tell me,' she said. 'Let me guess. The couple who couldn't decide who got the basketball season tickets finally settled it with shotguns at ten paces—'

'Oh, it's more exciting than that.' His voice was dry.

She sat up reluctantly. 'One of your clients is being beaten up by her ex-husband, and she's locked herself in the bedroom till you can rescue her?'

'No. Your sister and brother-in-law are at the gate.'

She blinked in astonishment. 'How?'

'I presume they finally gave in to the inevitable and rented a car, now that you're not providing one any more. Frankly, I don't care, but they will be here in about a minute and a half, so—'

'Why did you invite them in, Justin?'

He raised both eyebrows. 'Because they brought your cat.'

'You know what I mean.' It was quiet.

'Have you no feeling for the poor animal at all? Shelley implied that if we weren't

240

going to take him off her hands today, he might manage to get lost on his way back to the apartment. And may I suggest that you do not greet visitors in your present state of dress? I find it charming, but—'

She grabbed for her robe and clutched it to her chest.

'That makes a fetching picture,' he mused. He kissed her lightly. 'Don't look so terrified, Mac. We have to do this some time, you know.'

But not today, she thought. Not yet. Please, I just want a little time for the two of us first, to get used to things...

She gave a resigned little shrug. 'I just hope they aren't going to make a habit of it,' she said, under her breath. 'It's too much to bear.'

'I would say that's up to you,' he said unsympathetically.

The bell was ringing for the third time, with harsh impatience, when she pulled the front door open. Shelley thrust a box into her arms and stepped back to dust off her hands with a relieved sigh.

The box emitted a strident shriek, the

kind of protest that only a Siamese cat was capable of making.

'He's been doing that all the way across Phoenix,' Shelley said. 'I'm nearly deaf with the noise.'

'I'm not surprised that he's voicing his opinion,' Alisa said coldly. 'The poor darling is in misery, cramped into this little box. He has a travelling case, you know—'

'That doesn't explain why he howled all night,' Shelley went on. 'We didn't get a wink of sleep. You should be grateful we didn't turn up on your front step at five this morning with the little brat.'

'But we know how honeymooners are, so we waited till a civilised hour,' Clay murmured. 'At least, we assumed you'd be up by now.' There was a disagreeable note in his voice, and his eyes were intent on Alisa's face.

She didn't look at him. Why, she wondered in astonishment, didn't I ever before see the coarseness in him?

She knelt on the flagstone floor instead and opened the top of the box. Vibrato was huddled in the bottom of it, his cream-coloured body compressed into the smallest possible ball. He looked up at Alisa and wailed piteously.

'It's all right, darling,' she said. 'You can come out and start getting used to your new home.' He put a paw up to brush her hand, and she lifted him out and snuggled him against her shoulder.

'The rest of his stuff is in the car,' Shelley said with a shudder. She wandered back towards the sun-porch and looked into the library. 'It's not a bad house, Alisa,' she said in a congratulatory tone. 'Of course, it's a disaster at the moment, but that can be fixed with enough money.'

It was one thing, Alisa thought, to tally for herself how much work it would take to turn the house into a pleasant, homely space. But when Shelley began sneering at it...

Don't get vicious in return, she told herself. It won't gain you anything, and you'll feel rotten about losing your temper. She set Vibrato down carefully on the floor. He crouched into a watchful pose and began to inspect his new surroundings.

'And it's apparent that there's no lack of money,' Clay said under his breath. 'Which might account for a lot of things.'

Alisa ignored him, but it took an effort.

'Your apartment is really cute,' Shelley said, with an air of fairness. 'It's amazing what you've done with it. That's the other thing we wanted to talk to you about, Alisa. Since you'll have to pay out the lease for the next few months anyway, surely you wouldn't mind if we used it? We'll take care of the utility bills, of course.'

How generous, Alisa thought ironically. Not a word about the rent...

Vibrato moved cautiously across the hallway. From the corner of her eye Alisa could see him sniffing, then rubbing against, a friendly bare ankle. Justin had come in so quietly that she hadn't heard him. He was leaning against the arched doorway that led back towards the bedrooms.

She darted a glance at him. His face was non-committal. Obviously he was not going to step into this problem to rescue her, and she couldn't blame him for not wanting to be involved. But still... She gave him a pleading look.

'I'm sure we can work something out,' he said. 'A sub-lease, for instance.' But it's up to you, Alisa, he seemed to be whispering. How are you going to handle this? It's more than just the apartment, you know...

She grabbed at the suggestion with relief. 'Of course,' she said. 'I'd be happy to sub-let it for the same rent I've been paying.'

Shelley's mouth dropped open. 'But—'

Justin moved slightly. His face hadn't changed, and yet it seemed to Alisa as if he was applauding. 'I'll have someone in my firm draw up an agreement if you're interested,' he murmured. 'Sorry we can't ask you to stay for lunch, by the way—when you arrived, my wife had just reminded me that I've forgotten to restock the kitchen.'

The stunned looks on the faces of their guests made Alisa want to dissolve into hysterical laughter. The instant the door had closed behind them, she staggered into the library and threw herself down on her back on the leather couch, holding her sides and laughing as much from relief as from amusement.

Justin said, from the doorway, 'What are those noises you're making, Mac? Are you in pain?'

'No.' She gulped and wiped her eyes. 'Just thinking about their faces. Were they planning to walk over us forever, do you think?'

'Apparently so.' He sat down on the edge of the couch.

'Well, you stopped that in its tracks. Getting rid of them like that—' She sat up abruptly and threw her arms around him from behind, snuggling her cheek into the soft knit of his polo shirt just between his shoulder-blades. 'You're wonderful, Justin, do you know that? Absolutely wonderful. It's one of the things I—'

She stopped, because some still-watchful corner of her brain had ordered her throat to close up rather than to express the few brief, careless words that had so nearly escaped.

She closed her eyes and tried to swallow, and couldn't because her throat was too tightly constricted.

She had almost said, 'It's one of the things I love about you, Justin.'

CHAPTER NINE

It was only an idle thought, Alisa told herself in panic, not important at all. Nevertheless, it was an idle thought which would have caused all sorts of trouble if it had been expressed.

Your mouth has already got you into enough trouble, Alisa, she lectured herself. Isn't it about time you start watching what you say?

And why in heaven's name should that thought have bobbed to the top of her brain, anyway? It made no sense whatsoever; the workings of the subconscious mind were often ill-timed and embarrassing, but it generally managed to tell the truth. Whereas this—

'Time will teach thee soon the truth...'

She stirred uneasily. Where had that long-forgotten bit of verse come from? She hadn't read poetry for years. Besides, this

248

wasn't truth. It was romantic nonsense, born of wishful thinking, that was all. And yet, it had to have come from somewhere.

'One of the things I love about you, Justin.'

What in heaven's name was wrong with her? She couldn't be in love with him.

Why not? asked an uncomfortable little voice in the back of her brain.

Because what I felt for Clay was love, that's why, she argued.

Was it? the little voice nagged. And, even if it was, that's all over now. You were thinking only a minute ago that you were a fool not to have seen what Clay is really like—that doesn't sound much like love.

But that's got nothing to do with Justin, she told herself. It's out of the question to have fallen in love with him.

The little voice persisted, But you said, the two of you, that it wasn't love itself that was the fiction. You agreed that lasting love—real love—develops as people become friends and lovers and partners. You agreed that it might even happen to you in time.

But it couldn't have happened yet, she thought. Not yet.

Couldn't it have? the voice whispered. Perhaps it was already happening to you, before you ever thought of marrying him. Respect, admiration, liking, trust—you felt all those things. And now you know as well that he's the kind of sensitive, thoughtful lover that any woman could fall in love with—

Love, she thought. We're back to love again, dammit.

If you didn't love him, why did you marry him? the little voice taunted. You didn't have to. No one forced you. You could have stood up to Clay, and told him that if he bothered you again you'd tell Shelley everything. You didn't have to run to Justin for protection—

'That's one of the things...?' Justin prompted. He had turned to face her, and his fingers flicked carelessly across her cheek. 'What were you saying, Mac?'

Alisa looked down, concentrating on the tiny lines in the leather upholstery, afraid to meet his eyes. It was going to take time to sort out the confusion that was raging in her brain just now.

'That's one of the things I'm not very good at myself,' she whispered, only half hearing what she was saying. 'Asserting myself and refusing to let people walk over me.'

'I wouldn't say you're no good at it. You're certainly getting valuable practice. The bit about the rent was the turning-point, I think.'

She forced herself to laugh. 'As long as I'm practising asserting myself, how about letting me hire a housekeeper?'

He shifted his weight a bit and gently moved her into a half-reclining position on the couch. His hand slid softly over her hair, which was still damp from the pool and curling wildly as it began to dry. 'Would you really have wanted a housekeeper wandering around this morning?' he asked softly.

She shivered a little at the reminder; it had been very pleasant, out there by the pool, absolutely alone and free to do whatever they chose. 'Not exactly,' she whispered.

'Hire all the help you want, Mac. But make sure they're out of here on weekends, holidays, and evenings—all right?' His fingertips were trailing down her throat, tracing the low neckline of her knitted shirt. 'In the meantime, the house rule is that the last one to get up makes the bed. And you didn't.'

'That's the first I've heard about house rules.' She didn't make any move to slip from his arms; instead, she raised both hands to his face, using the tips of her index fingers to trace the outline of it. 'However, if you insist, I'll go and take care of it right now.'

'Just to show good faith, I'll help,' he suggested softly. 'I'm not a chauvinist about that sort of thing, you know. I think there are lots of things that should be shared.'

It was a softly sensual whisper. He took her hands and gently pulled her up from the couch, put an arm around her, and guided her back to the master suite. It was a long time before either of them remembered that they had set out to make the bed.

And as she lay in his arms, her senses still quivering from his lovemaking, Alisa admitted to herself almost with despair that the careless, thoughtless comment she had come so close to making had been the truth after all. Some time in the last few weeks the respect and liking that she had always felt for him had turned to love. At the same time that she had still clung to Clay—or at least to the image of him that she had adored—Justin had been creeping into her heart. That was why it had seemed so natural to turn to him, to seek him out, to share her problems. That was why she had married him; not to escape from Clay, or because he had promised money and ease, but because she had fallen in love with him, and she wanted to share his life. It was as simple as that.

And that left her squarely with a problem, for she could not tell him what she had discovered about her feelings.

Romantic love didn't work, he had said.

People fell out of love—no one could live at that peak forever... Most women would think that he would change his mind someday, but all her little romantic notions were removed long ago... That was really very lucky...

Now she had fallen in love, despite the warnings, despite the discussions, despite the reasonableness of all their arrangements. The mere hint of what she was thinking would be a crushing blow to him—perhaps he would see it as a betrayal of everything they had agreed to.

It was like suddenly awakening from a nightmare of walking a tightrope over a fathoms-deep canyon, only to find that the rope was real and the chasm was so deep that the bottom was not even in sight.

She turned in his arms and tipped her head back against his shoulder. He was watching her, with something in his eyes that was almost wariness, as if, she thought, he could sense the confusion inside her.

Or as if he was wondering if it had been Clay she'd been thinking of this time, as he'd made love to her.

The thought made her feel a little ill. She wanted to hold him close and reassure him that such a thing had not been in her mind, that she could not account for the aberration last night, and that he need not be concerned about it happening again, because she loved him instead.

I'm sure he'd find that very reassuring, Alisa told herself drily.

For a long instant she hovered on the brink of telling Justin the truth and taking the consequences. Then fear rose in her throat and silenced her. No, she thought. It isn't worth the risk. And telling him won't change how I feel. He was right; it would only make things uncomfortable. I can love him silently. I won't let it make any difference in our marriage, and so he'll never have to know that I haven't quite kept my end of the bargain...

When Ridge Coltrain came into her office on Thursday morning with a bulging briefcase, Alisa groaned. 'Not the Goulds again,' she said. 'I just finished typing up the whole mess!'

He grinned. 'No. In fact, I think they've actually agreed on two things—the property settlement, and the fact that they both hate their lawyers.'

'Most people do, by this stage,' Alisa said. 'You'll get used to it by the time you've handled a few more divorces.'

There were exceptions, of course, she reflected; one of them was in Justin's office right now. Debbie Baxter had been in there most of the morning, in fact, plotting a strategy to collect the back alimony she said her ex-husband owed her. She had obviously already heard about the weekend wedding, because she had greeted Alisa as 'Mrs Abernathy' with punctilious politeness and a cutting twist in her voice.

Ridge Coltrain perched on the corner of her desk and leaned across the blotter to get a better look at Alisa's ring. 'Nice,' he said. 'The grapevine has been very active about you all week, my girl.' He picked up her hand and turned it so the tsavorite garnet caught the light. 'I suppose this means you won't be looking for a job any time soon?'

The door of Justin's office opened and a vision in a pale yellow dress appeared on the threshold. Alisa swallowed a groan.

In slightly less than two seconds, Debbie had summed up the situation. 'Already holding hands with another man, Mrs Abernathy? I'd be careful about that sort of thing if I were you; it leaves the wrong impression in the office.'

Justin frowned. 'Dammit, Ridge, have you been trying to hire Mac away from me?'

Ridge smiled. 'Didn't you know? I thought that was why you were in such a hurry to marry her. Sorry, darling,' he told Alisa, in a stage whisper. 'I didn't mean to hurt your feelings, only his.'

She retrieved her hand with all the grace she could muster.

'You can't blame me for wanting to even the odds, Justin. Having access to all your secret strategies would help a lot. I've given up the idea, though,' Ridge admitted. 'I'd been having slightly less than no success in persuading her to resign, and now, of course—'

'Then why are you hanging around my office?' Justin asked.

'Because your chairs are much more comfortable than mine.'

'Then get off Mac's desk and come in where you can enjoy one of them,' Justin said crisply.

'I'll be in touch, Justin,' Debbie said softly, punctuating the remark with a manicured hand stroking the sleeve of his tweed jacket. She smirked a little at Alisa and left, her hips swaying in a sultry, enticing walk.

Justin watched her out of the office and then shook his head as if to clear it. 'She's obviously been watching too many old movies on late-night television,' he murmured.

'You're right. I couldn't quite place who she reminded me of this morning, but it was Marlene Dietrich,' Alisa murmured. 'I must say it makes a nice change from the all-American-girl personality—the tennis racket was getting tiresome.'

Justin smiled slowly. 'Are you being just a little vindictive, Mac? Shame.'

The smile was nearly her undoing. It caught at her throat, and sensual shivers seemed to radiate out from there till every cell in her body was remembering that he had smiled at her just that way last night, and then he had—

Stop it, she told herself. You're in an office, not a bedroom, and business is the order of the day. You don't see Justin forgetting that, and you'll just have to watch yourself.

She took a deep breath just as the office door started to close and said, 'Justin, I'm going to leave in half an hour to take Shelley and Clay to the airport.'

He stopped and turned in the doorway and looked at her thoughtfully. She held her breath. She hated having to break the peace of the last few days; they hadn't seen Shelley and Clay since Saturday, and this was the first time their names had even been mentioned.

Why didn't I just tell Shelley to call a damned cab? she asked herself furiously.

And yet—they had been her guests. Surely it was only good manners to say goodbye? When they came back in a week or two, to settle in permanently—well, that would be a little different.

'Why?' he asked lightly.

She was startled. 'They have to go back to Green Bay to clear up the details so they can move.'

'I meant, why are you taking them to the airport? I know why I'd have offered—to make sure they really leave town.'

'Justin, please. Shelley called this morning and asked if I would, and I thought it was the least I could do.' She felt as if she were stumbling over her tongue. 'I'll get someone in from the typing pool to answer the phone.'

He frowned, and for a moment she wondered if he was going to forbid her to go. 'Just make sure it's not the same one you got last time, Mac. We're going to have to do something right away about getting another secretary hired. I'd like to take you to Flagstaff with me next week, but unless we find someone...'

It might be only a business trip, with most of his time—and perhaps hers as well—tied up with legal details, but the promise of a week on the beach in Hawaii couldn't have made her any happier. 'I'll call the employment agency this afternoon, Justin.'

Ridge Coltrain's face appeared in the doorway. 'Justin, did I hear you say you're looking for a replacement for Alisa? Does that mean you'll be needing a job, my girl? I've got a wonderful opportunity for you—plenty of advancement possibilities, working for a rising young lawyer instead of this staid old firm—'

Justin planted a hand in the centre of Ridge's tie and gave him a playful push back into the office. 'Keep your sticky fingers off my secretary, Coltrain,' he warned mildly. 'I haven't fired her yet.'

Alisa bit her lip. Don't let it hurt you, she told herself. It doesn't really matter. No matter what he's feeling, Justin isn't the type to get sentimental in public. He's been as businesslike this week as ever—not a kiss, not even a touch, inside the office.

Of course he wouldn't make a real fuss about Ridge's teasing comment.

But she wished, in the most secret corners of her heart, that he had defended not his secretary, but his wife...

It was nearly a week later that her furniture arrived. The quantity of boxes and crates that filled the truck took hours to unload, and the crew was still working in the late afternoon when Justin's Cadillac pulled into the garage.

He strolled through the house, looking a little staggered at the change since he had left that morning. Then he released Vibrato from the bathroom, where the cat had been locked for safety's sake while the work proceeded, and carried him into the largest of the guest bedrooms, where Alisa was sitting cross-legged on the floor watching as one of the movers assembled her grandmother's carved walnut four-poster bed.

He stooped to kiss her, almost absent-mindedly. She interpreted the look in his eyes as shock, and said, 'Honestly, Justin,

I had no idea I owned so much stuff.'

The mover grinned. 'None of 'em do,' he said under his breath. He shouldered the tool kit and went back to the truck for another load.

Justin put a hand down and hauled Alisa to her feet. 'I knew I should have stopped at the gym instead of coming straight home,' he murmured, as they walked back to the living-room. 'Tell me, have you been collecting fabric samples long, or is this a new hobby?' He waved a hand at a wing-backed chair, where swatches had been tossed at random, filling the seat and cascading in a heap to the carpet. He put the cat down in the middle of the samples. Vibrato sniffed at them, pawed at Justin's arm, then—when he was ignored—snuggled down into the midst of the fabrics.

'Oh, the decorator was here today, too. I thought since I only had one day off I'd better make the most of it. How did your new secretary get along without me at the office today?'

Justin frowned. 'All right, but...'

Alisa tried to smother the tiny tinge of gladness that had sprung to life deep in her heart. It's silly to be glad that things didn't go smoothly, she told herself. But the truth is, she admitted, you don't want her to be too good! You're just a little bit afraid—a little insecure at the idea of someone taking the place you carved out. You'd like to be standing next to him every minute, just in case...

'She's got a lot to learn,' Justin said.

'It will take a while to train her. It's all right, Justin, I wasn't counting on going to Flagstaff with you tomorrow.'

He looked a little sheepish. 'You don't mind? It's not exactly an exciting trip, but...'

Yes, she thought. I mind. I don't want to go to work alone and then come home to this empty house. And it doesn't have to be an exciting trip; being with you is all the excitement I need.

But there would be other trips. She smiled a little, just thinking about all the possibilities the future held.

'I see you don't mind,' he said. 'I guess

it was pretty silly of me to think you might—Flagstaff can be a cheerless place in March.'

'It wasn't that,' she began, and then thought better of it. What was she going to tell him, after all—that she couldn't bear to be separated from him, that she loved him too much to let him go? That, she reminded herself, was scarcely the sort of thing their arrangement had allowed for. 'It will give me a chance to spread all these samples out and look them over,' she said casually. 'And then they will be out of your way.'

He cast a jaundiced glance at the pile, where Vibrato was snoozing with his paws shielding his eyes from the light. 'Work fast,' he said. 'I'm only going to be up there two days.'

The moving man returned, balancing a small swivel rocker. Alisa pointed out a spot by the fireplace, and he set it down.

'How much longer is this procession going to continue, Mac? It looks like the ceremonial interring of an ancient king of Egypt.'

'I think they're nearly finished. Why?'

'I had plans for tonight.' He moved aside as two men brought in an antique mahogany dining-table, then put his arms around her and rubbed his chin absently against the top of her head. 'A swim, then a nap, followed—unfortunately—by a little homework. I have to leave early in the morning. How about a nice quiet dinner at Emilio's?'

'That's quiet? I got steaks to broil, so we could initiate our dining-room.'

'Sure you want to cook after all this?'

'Of course,' Alisa said cheerfully. 'The men are doing all the work. Besides, if we don't have to drive all the way into town...' She locked her hands together at the nape of his neck and looked up, green eyes sparkling.

'Yes?'

'We'll have time for a longer nap,' she whispered.

He feigned shock. 'Mrs Abernathy, if I didn't know better I'd say I was just propositioned.' He followed her into the kitchen and made himself a glass of iced tea. Vibrato lazily climbed out of his nest and trailed after them, rubbing himself against Justin's ankles until he stooped and picked the animal up again. He stood by the chopping block in the centre of the room and scratched the cat's chin and looked thoughtfully around the kitchen, which was crammed with green plants. 'Did all these come out of your apartment?'

'No, but I've always thought there is nothing like a living thing to soften the outlines of a house, and now that I have room...' She waved a knife at the desk in the corner. 'Those go in the bay window in the dining-room, as soon as the movers clear out. The ones on the table get scattered around the rest of the house. And did you see the big ones on the sun-porch?'

'Bigger than these?'

She bit her lip and decided that a change of subject might be wise. 'I think that as soon as we're really settled we should have a party for the people from the law firm—a few of your clients, the judges and some of the other lawyers, perhaps.'

He made a doubtful-sounding noise.

'Don't worry; I'm not turning into a social butterfly, Justin,' she said. 'In fact, I'm a little nervous about it, but you really should be doing some entertaining.'

'You're right. But why be nervous? Everyone can wear tiger-skins and we can hand out machetes at the door.' She turned around to stare at him, but he appeared to be perfectly innocent. 'I think I'll go and hunt out a swimsuit.' He set the cat down and left the kitchen.

She caught up with him in the dining-room, where the last mahogany chair was, being carefully lined up against the table. 'Justin, are you really unhappy with what I'm doing? The furniture, the plants—everything? If you are...'

He looked down at her with one eyebrow raised.

'Perhaps I didn't really understand,' she whispered miserably. 'I didn't think I needed to check every detail out with you. And the house—Justin, it's important to me too that it be comfortable. You don't need to worry that I'm going to make it into some kind of museum—or a jungle, either! But I'm going to spend most of my time here, and I want it to be pretty, and pleasant, and inviting to our guests.'

He didn't say anything for a long moment, and when he did it wasn't what she had expected. 'I guess I just don't like all the confusion,' he mused. 'Once the messy part is over, I'll be all right.'

'I thought you liked clutter!'

He grinned, kissed her lightly on the nose, and vanished towards the master bedroom at the far end of the house.

Vibrato watched him out of sight and then stretched as far as he could, pawing at Alisa and pushing his little masked face against her hand to be petted. 'Don't come to me for sympathy when Justin walks out on you, you traitor,' she told him. 'I'm no fool. It's apparent you've already switched loyalties.' But she picked him up and started stroking his soft pale fur.

She was still a bit puzzled, but she tried to shrug it off. It will be all right as soon as the confusion is over, he had said, not quite sounding as if he believed it. But she told herself firmly that he was right, none the less. He would soon see that she was not going to dress his house in ruffled organdie, or fill it with antiques so precious that they couldn't be touched or used.

It will take a little time, that's all, she told herself. Lots of things just take time. It hasn't even been two weeks yet.

She was putting the steaks in a special marinade when the telephone rang, and she muttered a little curse under her breath at the hapless client who had to call at this hour. But it was not a client. It was Clay.

She was speechless for an instant, and he laughed, shortly. 'Surely you aren't surprised that I'd call as soon as I got back into town, Alisa? Not even the great lawyer could object to me letting you know that I made it.'

She looked over her shoulder, feeling a little guilty, as if Justin might be standing right behind her. 'I'm glad to know that you're back safely,' she said coolly. 'Give Shelley my best.'

'Shelley isn't with me.'

Alisa's heart seemed to melt into a quivering mass. 'What on earth do you mean?'

'What do you hope I mean?' It was soft and silky.

She shifted her grip on the telephone and said, 'Clay, don't be ridiculous. Why didn't she come with you?'

'Because she didn't want to spend four days in a car driving clear across the country, she said. She's planning to fly down next week.'

Alisa closed her eyes for an instant in relief.

'But I had four days to think about it all, Alisa. And that's the only thing I thought about as I made that long, miserable drive. I've decided I don't want her to come. You're right, darling. I was trying to have my cake and eat it, too. If you were trying to set me back on my heels and make me think, you got the job done.'

'I wasn't,' she said tautly.

But he didn't seem to hear. 'The sensible thing to do, it seems to me, is for Shelley to just stay in Green Bay, and let you and me—'

'No!' It seemed to burst from her throat. 'I am not interested in your plans, Clay. Not now, and not at any time in the future. I'm finished, do you hear me? I'm not going to listen to any more of this—'

'All right, I admit I was being a little crude before. It's worth whatever the divorce costs me, just to have it over with. Hell, she's welcome to everything. Then we can get married—that'll please you, won't it, darling?'

'Haven't you overlooked something? I'm married now, too.'

He laughed. 'Did you think that really bothered me? Alisa, it was a dumb-fool thing to do—trying to make me jealous that way. But it might work out all right in the long run. The settlement you'll get from him will make it a lot easier—'

'There wouldn't be a settlement under these conditions, Clay.' She hardly heard her own words. This is a nightmare, she told herself. It isn't really happening—I'm hallucinating.

My God, she thought. Last year I would have given anything to have Clay say these things to me. Now I just want it to stop. All I want is some peace, and a chance to make my marriage work. The last thing I need is for Clay to keep popping up again.

There was a brief silence, and then he said, 'Did you find out there is more money in Justin's pockets than you thought? Enough to make it worth your while to stay?'

'That has nothing to do with it, Clay.'

'But you've found yourself quite a cosy little nest there, haven't you? How would he like to have the details, do you think?' His voice was challenging. 'Shall I come out to the house tonight and we can discuss this—the three of us?'

'No!' She caught at her poise, but it was too late. 'He already knows about it, Clay. You couldn't shock him into kicking me out, if that's what you're trying to accomplish.' But Clay's mere presence would make things very unpleasant, she told herself. And he could be very suggestive. There was a sick feeling in the pit of her stomach; this could cost her any possibility of gaining the thing she wanted most in the world.

For more than a week she had been tiptoeing around the idea of love, pushing it to the back of her mind, pretending that it didn't matter that she had fallen in love with her husband, telling herself that whether he ever returned that love was a matter of no real concern. In truth she had been cherishing the hope that some day things would change and Justin would come to love her as she loved him.

But Justin thought that she was still half in love with Clay, and that her sense of honour and her love for her sister were all that had prevented her from throwing everything away in order to have him. The only way to convince him otherwise would be to confess her love for Justin himself—which was scarcely a better alternative, under the circumstances. And now Clay had risen up from the mists to threaten her again.

'He wouldn't happen to be standing next to you, telling you what to say, would he?' Clay speculated.

'I'm capable of making up my own mind about things like this. I'm quite serious, Clay. I've had enough of this situation—'

'But how do I know that?' he asked suspiciously. 'A couple of weeks ago you weren't telling me to get away from you. It seems plenty fishy to me that you've changed your mind so fast.'

'What will it take to convince you that I mean what I say?' Alisa asked drily. 'I could just tell Shelley everything, you know—'

'Tell me instead, face to face,' he said promptly. 'Without the great lawyer along to twist things around. You can lie over the telephone, Alisa, but your eyes can't lie to me. That's how I knew you were still in love with me the minute I stepped off the plane, you know.'

Her throat was too tight to speak.

'Look me in the face and tell me, if you

can,' he said. 'And if you can't, then I'll know.'

You have to do something, she told herself desperately. You can't just let this go on. Somehow you have to make Clay believe that you mean it, that you don't want to have anything more to do with him. And if seeing him once more is what it takes...

'What about that little French restaurant in the hotel?' Clay said. 'It should be quiet enough.'

She protested automatically. 'Not in public, Clay.' But actually, she thought, it was too quiet; it might be technically a public place, but it was still a hideaway. The kind of people who went there were the ones who knew Justin, and it was certainly no place for a discussion that might end up in shouting. But what else was she to do? She could scarcely allow him to come to the house. She wouldn't feel quite safe alone with him, and if that was what he insisted on, to be convinced that she was through—

'Alisa?' Clay said, with a challenge in his

voice. 'Surely you can manage to escape from him to see me? Or I can follow you around till you're alone.'

'All right,' she said. 'One o'clock tomorrow, outside the French restaurant.' She put the telephone down abruptly.

At least I've bought myself some time, she thought. Perhaps by tomorrow I can think of a better way.

Finally her hands stopped trembling, and she was turning the steaks in the marinade when Justin came in, wearing a terry robe. 'Still at it?' he asked lightly. 'Come out and have a swim. The movers are all finished and gone, thank God.' He refilled his tall glass with ice and tea.

For the tiniest part of a moment, she contemplated telling him. But what good would that do? It wasn't as if he could do anything to solve the problem. This one is up to you, Alisa, she told herself. If Justin steps in, it will only make matters worse. And what could he do, anyway? She realised belatedly that she didn't even know where Clay was staying, or how to reach him.

I'll tell Justin as soon as he gets back, she promised herself. It's not that I'm trying to keep anything secret. There's just no point in him worrying about it, when he'll be in Flagstaff...

Or would she tell him? He had said long ago that he considered the matter past, fit only for forgetting. Why bring it up again? She could deal with it by herself, and then she could forget it all, too.

'I don't really feel like a swim,' she said. 'But I'll come out for a while before I cook the steaks.' The sky was beginning to darken as she threw herself down in a lounge chair beside the pool and tried to relax. It looked like a storm was building far to the west, for the clouds had turned almost wine-coloured, but overhead, beyond the palm trees that sheltered the pool, the sky was still clear.

He was looking at her a bit oddly. 'You will be all right while I'm gone, won't you, Alisa? You're not afraid to stay alone?'

'Of course I'm not.'

'I'll call you at the office tomorrow.'

She tried to sound careless. 'I might

take a friend out to lunch. Or I might go shopping instead. I forgot to tell you—I got a telephone call from Great-Aunt Louise today.'

He paused on the edge of the pool, obviously astonished. 'You're joking?'

'Well, indirectly, at least. It was the crystal department at the Tyler-Royale store, actually. She'd sent them a telegram telling them to let us choose whichever pattern we wanted and give us twelve of everything and send her the bill.'

He whistled. 'And you were worried because we didn't get a letter from her last Friday, or any acknowledgement of our announcement,' he chided. 'I'd say Great-Aunt Louise considers you an official member of the family now.' He saluted solemnly, and dived back into the pool to finish his laps.

By the time he returned to sit beside her, the evening star had appeared. She had put her head back to stare up at it, as if it held some sort of secret, if she could only read its mystery.

Justin followed her gaze. 'Venus,' he said

thoughtfully. 'The planet of lovers.'

There was a brief, poignant silence. She almost told him, then, that she loved him, almost threw caution to the winds in the hope that her love would make everything all right. Perhaps she would have, if he had only turned his head and smiled at her. But instead he looked up at the tiny, glowing white speck and added wryly, 'The atmosphere there is inhospitably hot and poisonous to breathe, I understand. That's very appropriate, don't you think?'

There was a bitter taste in her throat, a sadness that came from wishing that there really could be nothing but truth between them. But she herself had messed that up, when she had crossed the line between respect and love, and made it necessary to hide an essential bit of herself from the man she loved.

'Yes,' she said quietly. 'It's very fitting indeed.'

CHAPTER TEN

Justin's nap was forgotten in favour of an hour in his library, and after dinner he retreated there again, his mind occupied by the depositions he would be taking tomorrow in Flagstaff. Alisa wasn't surprised; she had heard him say more than once that the only conflict which was longer and more complicated than the average divorce was chess-by-mail, while the usual petty boundary war between two countries was usually far more quickly negotiated than the battle between spouses.

She spent the evening in the kitchen, cleaning up the mess, arranging plants in the bay window in the dining-room, and unpacking the boxes that the movers had brought. It was mindless work, but it kept her hands busy.

It was after midnight when Justin came in to say goodnight, and she was startled to see the time. She waved a hand at the box she had just opened and said, 'I think I'll finish this before I come to bed, if you don't mind.'

He gave her a tired half-smile and said, 'Just as well if you do. I'd better be on the road by six o'clock.' He kissed her lightly and left her there, surrounded by packing debris.

I'm glad I didn't tell him about Clay, she thought, as she plunged into the mess again. He has enough on his mind.

Venus had long since dropped below the horizon, and the stars were beginning to fade, when she fixed the coffee-pot, plugging it into a timer so it would start itself. It would be a quick breakfast, but at least she could send him off warm and alert, with an extra cup to drink along the way.

Alisa, your conscience is nagging at you, she told herself.

He was sound asleep, sprawled on his back in the exact centre of the big bed. She crept in beside him and curled up against his warmth, and he turned over and draped an arm across her precisely as if she were a teddy bear. It was comforting to be held, and in a matter of minutes, soothed by the slow rhythm of his breathing, she was asleep too.

In the morning, when she woke, he was already gone. The coffee-pot was empty and the vacuum bottle she had left beside it was missing; on the butcher's block in the centre of the kitchen was a note.

'I couldn't wake you,' it said. 'I'd rather take with me the memory of you sleeping.'

She put it down, not quite certain whether she was pleased by his thoughtfulness or annoyed by her missed opportunity. She turned to make herself a fresh cup of coffee. He had refilled the pot and plugged it in, but he hadn't reset the timer, so the machine was just sitting there, patiently waiting for further instructions. Poor Justin, she thought with a smile. He was so totally non-mechanical!

Supervising the new secretary took only a fraction of Alisa's attention; the woman had ten years of experience and a solid grasp of the fundamentals. She needed only time to understand how Justin liked things done, and to familiarise herself with all the cases that were in progress.

The result was that Alisa had plenty of time to think about her own problem that morning. Plenty of time to watch with dread as the clock's hands inched around towards one o'clock. Plenty of time to consider all the possible results of a luncheon with Clay. Plenty of time to scold herself for ever agreeing to meet him.

What possible good would it do? she asked herself. If he hadn't believed her over the telephone, why would he be convinced when she said the same things in person? Indeed, the opposite was more likely; he was quite capable of convincing himself, because she had agreed to meet him, that things were just as they had always been.

But she didn't know what to do instead. Why didn't I tell Justin? she thought helplessly as noon approached. He might have been annoyed, perhaps even angry, but he would have given me some good solid legal advice, despite his own feelings.

She looked at the telephone, but she knew there was no way to reach him now. He would already be closeted in some little office, concentrating on digging out the financial facts about a broken marriage. She had waited too long; not even the brand-new telephone in his car would do her any good just now.

But if she had asked him for advice, what would he have told her? Come on, Alisa, she ordered herself. Figure it out—you should be able to, after eight months of working with him. What would he have said to a client who found herself in this position?

She shifted the pile of paperwork that she had spread out on the blotter on Justin's desk and rolled a pen between her fingertips. Then she pulled a sheet of his stationery out of the drawer and started to write.

The main lobby of the Kendrick Hotel was a kaleidoscope of colours and patterns as guests checked in, checked out, wandered between the pool and the gift shop, searched out the meeting rooms and the bar. The tourists' bright summery clothes contrasted with the businessmen's sober pin-striped suits and the staff's desert-tan uniforms, all against the background of the lush green plants that turned the lobby into an inviting garden. Alisa purposely kept her eyes straight ahead as she crossed to the quieter side lobby where the French restaurant was located; if she didn't see anyone, she reasoned, she wouldn't have to greet them or explain why she was there. She was, intentionally, fifteen minutes early. She had no intention of staying a moment longer than necessary.

She chose a chair in a discreet corner just outside the restaurant, screened by a big potted tropical palm which allowed her to see the passing crowd without being seen. She kept her handbag in her lap, and now and then her fingertips crept into the side pocket to make sure that the fat white envelope was still there. The moment that Clay appeared she would give it to him, and then she could leave all this behind.

It was nearly one o'clock when a bell-boy

materialised next to her chair. 'Ma'am? You were to meet a gentleman here?'

She nodded, and her fingers stilled against the linen-like finish of the envelope.

'He asked me to give you this.' He dropped something into her hand, gave her a brisk half-salute and a professional smile, and disappeared before she could gather her wits.

The object was a bit of pasteboard, shaped like a credit card and perforated with rows of neatly punched holes. It was a room key, of the style favoured by many new hotels.

I should have expected something of the sort, Alisa thought wearily.

Her first impulse was to bury the key in the sand in the nearest ashtray and then walk out, but a moment later anger began to consume any common sense she had left. She was furious at the way he was manipulating her, and determined that it was not going to go on, and so she gritted her teeth and said, under her breath, 'This is going to end, right now.'

The room key directed her to the

mezzanine floor, where balconies over-looked the pool and the big lobby. Heavy curtains were drawn across the glass doors of the room; it was impossible to see even whether the lights were on inside. She knocked, but there was no answer, and finally, reluctantly, she used the key.

Perhaps it's better this way, she thought. I'll leave the letter where he can't miss it, and then I'll get out, before anything else can happen.

The door swung silently open. The room was almost dark; all the curtains were drawn, and none of the lamps had been turned on. She let the door close softly behind her and stood silently for a moment, waiting for her eyes to adjust to the dimness. It was a small suite, she saw; she was in the sitting-room section. The chairs and the love-seat were only shadowy outlines.

There was a tiny movement in the gloom off to her left, where a dark doorway yawned. She spun around to face it and said, firmly, 'Once and for all, Clay, I'm finished with these stupid games. Now I'm going to make the rules.'

There was no answer, just a tiny click followed instantly by a rush of light that nearly blinded her. The sudden shock of it sent her reeling, making her lean for support against the back of a chair. But the second blow, the one that struck her a split-second after the light came on, was worse.

'Just what sort of rules are you going to make, Alisa?' a voice asked softly, and Justin came slowly, inexorably, across the room towards her.

'What are you doing here?' she began weakly. 'You're supposed to be in Flag-staff—' She bit her tongue hard, knowing that, in her shock, she must sound as guilty as any woman could possibly be.

He shrugged. 'My plans changed,' he said coolly. 'Sorry I didn't have the chance to let you know. I am glad you could join me, however—instead of spending the afternoon with Clay.'

'I wasn't planning to spend the afternoon with him,' she began furiously. 'And how the hell...?' She stumbled to a stop.

'What you really want to ask is, how did I know that you were meeting your lover.'

She shook her head. 'Justin, I—' She wet her lips and tried again. 'This isn't what you think it is. We agreed to meet in the restaurant—'

'Now that is certainly odd. I checked, you see, and there was no reservation made in your name, or in his. I didn't think to ask about "Mr and Mrs John Doe"—should I have, Alisa?'

There was an almost metallic hardness to his voice, the same tone she had heard sometimes when he'd been pounding questions at an uncooperative witness, and it terrified her.

'Has it occurred to you that there might be an innocent explanation of that?'

'You certainly didn't hesitate to use that key. It seemed to me that you expected to be invited upstairs—'

'That doesn't make sense, you know. Even if you're so determined to think the worst of me, how do you account for the fact that I was sitting in the lobby?' It was a challenge, flung at him. 'Why didn't he just give me his room number?'

'Because he registered only this morning. He didn't have the room number last night when he called you.'

The words dropped into the sudden stillness of the room like a boulder into the centre of a lily pond, and the resulting ripples threatened to rock Alisa off her feet. 'So that's how you knew. You listened in on my call,' she began furiously. But he couldn't have heard it all, she realised, or he would have known that this meeting hadn't been her idea, that she had been left with little choice... She tried to gather her scattered poise.

'It's very wise of you not to make a fuss about that, considering the circumstances. As a matter of fact, I didn't set out to spy on you. I was just coming to the kitchen to get another glass of tea, and I happened to hear a bit of your conversation—a few words that interested me a great deal. So I listened. And then I knew why you hadn't been anxious to come to Flagstaff with me after all.'

She turned her back on him and stood

with her shoulders hunched, her knuckles pressed against her teeth. She was caught in a web that she had spun all by herself, a web from which there was no escape. Whatever she said now, whatever she did, he would not believe her. And she couldn't blame him. She had sprung this trap on herself, in her idiotic desire to protect herself—and him—from pain...

'And even then I wanted to trust you,' he said, sounding thoughtful.

She made one last, desperate attempt at convincing him. 'Is this an example of what you call *trust?* Hearing a few words—half of a conversation—and drawing this sort of conclusion from it?'

'I didn't imagine you telling Clay to meet you outside the restaurant, Alisa.' His voice was harsh. 'And I didn't imagine it a little later, when you told me about your plans to take a friend to lunch today—'

'I made you a solemn promise—'

'You lied to me about your lunch date,' he said quietly. 'Is that what your promise is worth?'

It was like a diamond-edged dagger,

razor-sharp, carving fragments from her heart. Bitterness rose up inside her. Her hands fluttered in a frustrated, futile, hopeless gesture. He was correct, after all—she had lied. And because she had, anything else she might say would be suspect.

'I suppose Clay is going to appear at any minute,' she said. 'Just to top off the situation.'

'Oh, no. This isn't his room, you know—I'm paying the bill. And I didn't invite him to join the party.'

'I should have known.' She cast a scathing glance around the sitting-room. This must be one of the more desirable suites in a hotel that was not known for bargain rates; Clay would never think of spending so much money on a room, no matter what sort of rendezvous he had planned. The last hope she had held—that, even if she could not convince Justin, she might still be able to force Clay to tell the truth—vanished. 'Well, if it's not a confrontation that you're after, then what is it?'

'You came here to spend the afternoon with your lover, Alisa,' he said, with a silky innuendo. 'I'd hate for you to be cheated altogether—but you'll have to accept me as a substitute, I'm afraid.' He pulled his tie loose and flung it aside, and tossed his jacket over the arm of a chair.

She was too stunned to move. Not Justin, she thought. Not this...

She backed away from him instinctively. He was between her and the doorway, advancing purposefully. She bumped into a chair and stumbled, and he seized her. He took her handbag from her arms, where she was clutching it as if it was some kind of shield, and threw it over his shoulder and halfway across the room.

She tried to kick him in the shin and missed. He swore and picked her up bodily, tossing her over his shoulder to carry her into the bedroom next door. She pounded her fists against his shoulders, but she might have been an insect for all the attention he paid to the assault; he turned the lights on and pulled the satin bedspread back, as casually as if her writhing body across his shoulder was nothing at all. Then he flung her down on the bed and held her there with his own weight when she tried to wriggle free. She had always known that he was strong, but it terrified her to know that he was capable of using that strength as a weapon.

With her last bit of breath, the last ounce of courage, she spat, 'You'll have to beat me.'

'No,' he whispered. 'There are better ways to wipe him out of your mind, Alisa.'

She turned her head, and his mouth brushed against her throat, scorching the soft skin.

'You don't need to worry about that,' she said bitterly. 'I can't fool myself into thinking you're him, Justin, no matter how hard I pretend. Do you think I could ever forget what you've taught me this afternoon? I'll go to my grave remembering what you've done to me today, and hating you for it.'

The words echoed—or was it only in her brain that the repetition sounded, over and over—and for an instant time itself seemed to stop as everything hung in the balance.

With a muttered oath, he rolled away from her and lay on his back, his breath rasping, one forearm across his face. She scrambled off the bed, trembling violently; the ability to think logically was long gone. She tripped over her handbag on the sitting-room carpet and mindlessly stooped to pick it up. It wasn't until she was in the lobby again that she even realised she had it, and then she breathed a wordless little sigh of relief and fumbled in the depths of it for her car keys.

A hand came to rest on her arm just above the elbow, and she spun around and stamped the pointed heel of her shoe down as hard as she could on the instep of the man who stood beside her. The impact sent a sharp jolt through her ankle.

Clay let out a strangled yelp and jerked away, holding his wounded foot in the air. 'Dammit, Alisa!'

She blinked in astonishment, but an instant later she was back in control.

'You!' she said with loathing. 'Don't you ever touch me again, Clay—or telephone me, or send me a message. In fact, don't be surprised if I start to scream if you ever come within sight of me again. And if you need to have it put any more plainly, there are judges who will make a court order of it!'

He looked stunned, and he still hadn't found his voice when she turned her back on him, heedless of the interested bystanders in the lobby, and stalked out to her car. She sank down gratefully behind the wheel and tried to figure out what came next.

In the end, she went back to the house. She would gather up a few necessary things and go—somewhere, she thought helplessly. Where *did* people go, anyway, when they couldn't stand to be together any more? she wondered, and remembered that the previous owners of this house had waited out the last few months of their dying marriage separated only by a concrete driveway. Too bad Justin hadn't bought the recreational vehicle from them too, she thought, and burst into half-hysterical laughter. It would be only fitting for one of us to move into it.

Her ankle was aching by the time she reached the house, and she limped into the living-room and dropped into the swivel rocker beside the fireplace. It was the rocker she had intended to re-upholster in a blue and mauve check, to co-ordinate with the muted chintz that she was going to use on Justin's love-seat. The fabric swatch was lying across the arm of the chair. She had chosen it just this morning, before she went to work...

Tears stung her eyes. Time, she thought bitterly. I thought that all it would take was a little time. For the house, and for us as well. I was so certain it would all work out.

But now all those hopes had ended in nothingness, like the residue of the last log that still lay in the fireplace. The grey ash was like a ghost of the original; it still held the shape of the log, but the merest touch would reduce it to dust, she thought, just as her hopes had been reduced and exposed as the illusions they were. Just like her love for Justin...

No, she admitted painfully, that hadn't turned to ashes. It was still there, alive and throbbing and begging for sustenance, despite everything that had happened between them.

It will go away, she told herself. Love can't last long where there isn't trust, and respect.

Vibrato came in, silent-footed, from somewhere in the far reaches of the house. He stretched and yawned and leaped up into her lap, snuggling down under her hand and licking her fingers. It was the final blow to her composure. She bent her head over him, and a tear or two dropped on to the soft fur.

She didn't know how long she sat there, with the cat's rasping purr shutting out everything else. But eventually a sort of prickling on the back of her neck warned her that she was no longer alone, and she jerked her head up away from the cat's soft fur to look over her shoulder.

She jumped to her feet, and her ankle

shrieked in protest. A wave of nauseating pain swept over her, and she collapsed into the chair again, holding her ankle, rocking herself in a vain attempt to soothe the ache, with tears streaming down her face.

Justin came quietly across the room. 'Let me look at it.'

She shook her head defiantly. 'I twisted it that's all.'

He stood and looked down at her for a long moment and then turned on his heel. A couple of minutes later, when he came back with an icepack, she was standing up again, trying tentatively to put her weight on the weak ankle.

'Sit down,' he ordered. 'Or I'll put you in that chair.'

She sat. 'Don't worry,' she said snidely. 'I haven't forgotten that you're stronger than I am. You proved that much this afternoon—if nothing else.'

His face went white under the tan, and she saw his fingers clench for a moment on the icepack. He knelt beside her, and his hands were gentle as he probed the joint and then wrapped the ice around it.

'I don't think you've broken it,' he said quietly.

She studied his face, seeking something —she didn't quite know what. She was searching for a clue as to what he was thinking. If there was the least sign that he really cared, surely she would be able to see it now?

But there was nothing, and with a sigh she let her gaze drop to his hands, strong and brown, still holding the ice tightly against her ankle. The cat rubbed himself against Justin's wrist and jumped back in offended surprise when his nose touched the cold pack.

'I've always prided myself on my legal logic,' he mused. 'I found out today that it doesn't always carry over into real life.'

'Congratulations,' she said tartly.

'There is no excuse for what I did today, Alisa. Assaulting you like that—' He shook his head. 'I had no idea I was capable of behaving so badly.'

'To say nothing of the fact that an assault charge could have got you disbarred,' she agreed in a tight little monotone.

His eyes seemed to flicker a little, but his voice was steady. 'I suppose there's no point in saying that I wish it hadn't happened.'

'Look on the positive side,' she recommended. 'Perhaps it will make you a little more understanding of your clients' foibles. The next time one of them descends to violence—'

'Perhaps. At any rate, for whatever good it does, I humbly beg your pardon.'

'You never did anything humbly in your life, Justin.' She leaned her head against the back of the chair and closed her eyes. 'You're arrogant and self-assured and egotistical—your entire approach to marriage is an outrage, and why I ever got tangled up in it is beyond my understanding.' Be honest with yourself at least, she thought. You were certain—even then—that you could change him.

'You're quite correct,' he said quietly. 'It isn't very pleasant to have to admit that I've been totally and horribly wrong, Alisa.'

And that, she thought wearily, is the end of that.

She moved her ankle, experimentally, and realised that he was still clutching the icepack. 'You must be freezing your fingers.'

'I want to keep the ice tightly against the joint.'

Of course, she thought dully. Because as soon as she could walk on it—well, she didn't want him to have to carry her out to her car, any more than he wanted to.

'I still don't understand,' she said painfully. 'Why didn't you say something —do something—last night? Why did you wait, and let all this happen?'

For a long moment she thought he wasn't going to answer. Finally he sighed, heavily, and said, 'Because I hoped it would come to nothing—that you would reconsider, and decide not to go. Don't you see, Alisa? Then I would never have had to admit that I knew, and there wouldn't have been a fuss.'

'And you'd have had a secret weapon to hold over me forever,' she said drily.

'That didn't occur to me.'

'But something changed your mind.'

'The longer I thought about it, the more this little voice at the back of my brain told me that you weren't going to change your mind about seeing him.'

'Justin—'

'I kept trying to tell myself that even if you saw him, it didn't mean that it was important. And yet—I kept remembering that you didn't need to spin me the story about taking a friend to lunch, but you had done so. That surely meant you had something to hide.'

She made a tiny wordless protest.

He shook his head. 'Alisa, I'm just telling you how my mind was working. I didn't want you to lie to me any more—so I didn't wake you this morning. But the further I drove—'

'Then you did go to Flagstaff?'

He gave her a tiny, twisted smile. 'About halfway. I had nothing but time to think, while I drove, and that little voice kept telling me that I was being played for a fool. I had to know, don't you see? Whether you saw him or not, whatever you did—I had to know. So I cancelled my appointment and came back—and I found out that there were no reservations at the restaurant, but that Clay had checked into the hotel this morning, without his wife, and ordered a bottle of champagne brought upstairs—'

'And you thought that meant I was a willing participant.'

He didn't look at her. 'It looked damned plain, Alisa. Still, it was only circumstantial evidence. I decided to give you all the rope you needed to hang yourself, so I rented the suite, and sent the bell-boy down with the key—'

'And I walked right into the trap, didn't I?' she said bitterly.

'When you took the key and came upstairs—almost eagerly—something inside me exploded,' he admitted quietly. 'Alisa, I've never done anything like that in my life. I didn't know I was capable of losing all reason, of letting my temper rule me—'

'Well, now we both know.' She shifted uncomfortably in the chair and tried to rotate her ankle again. It was better, she thought, but was that only the ice, numbing the pain?

'If it isn't better in a couple of hours,' Justin said, 'I'll take you over to the clinic to have it X-rayed, just to be certain.'

She stared at him, her green eyes wide, speechless with shock. It hadn't seemed to occur to him that in a couple of hours she was going to be far away. Unless...

Could he possibly mean that, after everything that had happened between them this afternoon, he still expected that there would be no divorce?

Then he's a fool, she thought. Without trust and honesty between us, there would never again be peace, comfort, serenity—the things that make life bearable. I can live without his love if I have to, she told herself, but not without his trust. And he had made it cruelly apparent that he had not been able to trust her.

'I'm leaving, Justin. Whether my ankle is better or not, I'm leaving—'

'You don't need to be afraid of me.' It was quiet, almost lifeless. 'Not any more.' A moment later, he added, sounding almost curious, 'Why haven't you tried to explain, Alisa? To defend yourself?'

The last whisper of hope died, then. Nothing would change it; nothing would convince him. And even if there was some evidence—

But there was; there was the letter she had written to Clay. She hadn't remembered it, in that brief clash in the hotel lobby. It was still in her handbag.

But she didn't reach for it. If he trusted me, he would believe what I say, with or without the letter, she thought. But he doesn't, and the letter won't change that. I could have written it this afternoon; it, too, could be a lie.

'Does it matter any more?' she asked quietly.

His eyes fell. 'Perhaps it doesn't.' His hands slipped from the icepack.

She stood up, tentatively. The ankle still hurt, but it held her weight. She leaned against the back of a chair to help take the strain off it.

How, she wondered, did one actually say goodbye? How were the loose ends

307

to be handled, the mundane details of the legal paperwork and the things she was leaving behind? She had helped to arrange the minutiae of a thousand dying marriages, but when it was her own she was helpless.

He had stood up, too. He had picked up Vibrato. 'What about the cat?'

'Why? Are we going to have a custody battle over him?'

'I meant, are you taking him today— that's all?'

'No,' Alisa said coolly. 'I'm sure the Kendrick Hotel doesn't allow pets.'

Justin's fingers stroked the pale fur. 'Why do you want me to believe that you're going to join Clay, Alisa?'

For an instant she wasn't sure she had heard him correctly. Then she half turned, and said, 'Isn't that what you think?' She wanted it to be crisp, polite. Instead, it came out as a weak little whisper.

He shook his head. 'I couldn't hear what you said to him in the lobby, but the look on his face made it apparent what the message was. And when I found this on the floor in the suite...' He held out a fat white envelope. 'It must have fallen out of your handbag. I read it,' he admitted. 'It wasn't sealed.'

She was trembling. 'Then why did you let me think you still believed that I—' She stumbled over her tongue. She closed her eyes and took half a dozen shallow breaths. 'Why didn't you tell me that you knew I wasn't there to have an affair with him?'

'Didn't I? In any case, you said it didn't matter, that what I did this afternoon was too awful to forgive.'

She shook her head, blindly.

'That's not what you said?' He sounded as if all the breath had been knocked out of him.

She was swaying a little. He dropped the cat. In two steps he was beside her, his arm closing around her to support her and take her weight against him. 'Alisa, is it too awful to forgive?'

'It depends,' she said. 'Why did you do it?'

'I should have trusted you. I did trust

you, until my blind, stupid, jealous rage took over—'

'Justin!' It was only a whisper, really—of shock, of faintly dawning hope.

He looked down into her eyes and muttered something under his breath. Then he lifted her bodily off her feet and sat down in the chair with her in his lap, holding her tightly as if he was afraid that she would jump up and run.

'I thought it wouldn't matter, that you still loved him,' he said, as if the words were being forced from him. 'We had made a bargain, and your feelings for Clay had nothing to do with it. But it wasn't enough, Alisa. The night I made love to you, and you called his name—I told myself it didn't matter, that you were my wife, that you had put him out of your life, and sooner or later you'd stop thinking about him, too. But I found myself wanting more than that. I wanted to wipe him out of your memory. I couldn't forget, you see, that you would never have married me if he had been free.'

Her head was swimming a little; she put

it down against his shoulder. 'It would have been very unlucky for me if I had married him.'

'Yes, common sense should have told you that. But common sense isn't really very common,' Justin said wryly. 'Then I heard you arranging to meet him, and I think right then I went over the brink. I was terrified of losing you, so terrified that for the first time in my life I was afraid to fight for what I wanted. That's why I left you sleeping this morning. I was afraid that you wouldn't be here when I came home, and I wanted that picture of you—peaceful, contented, in my arms—to carry with me. I didn't want to see you awake and happy, and trying to hide it because it was Clay who made you feel that way.'

She could scarcely breathe. She wanted to pinch herself to be certain that she was awake, but she was afraid to move. 'And so I ended up crushing the very thing that is most precious to me,' he admitted huskily. 'When I came out of my jealous fury this afternoon long enough to realise that I had convicted you without proof—and that

I had been horribly wrong—all I could remember was your saying you would hate me forever for what I'd done.'

She put her arms around him and turned her face into his neck, and two hot tears sank silently into his collar.

'Alisa,' he whispered, 'was it only the promise you gave me that made you tell him to leave you alone?'

She shook her head, and his hand crept to the nape of her neck to stroke the soft blonde hair. His fingers trembled a little.

'I didn't think you'd believe me,' she confessed softly. 'Or worse, I thought you'd feel that I'd broken our bargain.'

'Why? I don't understand—'

'If I told you I loved you,' she whispered.

His arms tightened around her until she thought every bone in her body was going to be squeezed into sand. 'So much for all our fine theories.'

'Your theories, don't you mean? I don't think I ever truly believed all that nonsense.'

'Well, I did. I know, now, that no other woman would have done—if you hadn't agreed to marry me I'd have looked forever. But admitting that I'd fallen in love with you didn't come easy, Alisa. It violated every rule I had ever made for myself, every conviction I'd ever held. I could scarcely keep on jeering at the idea of one perfect love when I'd found mine. And I couldn't even tell her that I'd found her, because she loved someone else, and not me at all—'

She shook her head. 'Oh, I love you all right,' she said. 'You're not my one perfect love, that's true—you're an imperfect one at best—but still...'

He laughed ruefully. 'I'm afraid that's the best I can do, Mac. But I'll try.' His mouth came down on hers with dizzying certainty, and Alisa's insides began to squirm.

'I'll settle for it,' she said breathlessly, when he finally raised his head.

He only smiled and ran a fingertip down the front of her blouse. She hadn't realised that his hands had been busy, but suddenly the blouse gaped open, and an instant later he had unfastened the front of her bra and his palm was caressing her breast, sending a surging ache of longing through her that made her gasp and press herself closer against him, as she had thought she could never do again.

They made love in front of the empty fireplace, slowly, gently, soothingly, and the pain they had suffered separately faded and healed and left them clinging to each other.

Later, he built a fire, and when it was crackling merrily he came back to snuggle down beside her. 'How does your ankle feel?'

'What ankle?' she asked, watching the leaping flames. 'Oh. It stopped hurting long ago. I wonder if Clay's foot has.'

'Is that how you hurt it? That must have happened before I got to the balcony.' He sounded only mildly interested. 'Your voice is like sun-warmed sandpaper, Mac.' His was muffled; he was nibbling at the lobe of her ear.

'I think,' she announced dreamily, 'that I'm going to name our first son Mac.'

For a long time he didn't say anything

at all, but eventually, reluctantly, he gave up his investigation of the sensitive spot at the base of her throat and raised himself on one elbow to look down at her. 'Why would you want to do a damn-fool thing like that?'

'Because then, to avoid confusion, you'd have to stop calling *me* Mac.'

'Oh.' He started nibbling again, this time sampling the soft valley between her breasts. 'Do you really hate it so very much—Mac?' he whispered. His fingers wandered, apparently aimlessly, over her flat stomach, across the outline of her hip, to caress the satin skin of her inner thigh.

The ripple of pleasure that was running through her veins was steadily increasing into a torrent. 'Not—not when you're doing that,' she confessed, a little shakily.

Justin raised his head and smiled. 'You're quite certain you don't object?'

She arched her body against him, with a wordless little cry.

'That's what I thought,' he murmured. 'So I plan to go right on doing it, Mac. Forever—if not a little longer.'

This Large Print Book for the Partially sighted, who cannot read normal print, is published under the auspices of

THE ULVERSCROFT FOUNDATION